TARGET RISK

John Wingate

SAPERE
BOOKS

TARGET RISK

Published by Sapere Books.

20 Windermere Drive, Leeds, England, LS17 7UZ,
United Kingdom

saperebooks.com

ISBN: 978-1-80055-455-9

Progress is the law of life, man is not man as yet.
Robert Browning: *Paracelsus*

ACKNOWLEDGEMENTS

I wish to thank those many friends and acquaintances who gave me so much help and time, who proffered their advice and encouragement. I encountered kindness from people in every sphere of life, men and women who gave freely of their experience and goodwill; I wish to thank them, though they are too numerous to name individually. I hope they will bear with my unintended discourtesy.

My gratitude is particularly due to: Mr Julian Faber, Chairman of Willis, Faber and Dumas Ltd; Mr James Aarvold, of Willis, Faber and Dumas Ltd; Mr Derry Nicolson, Editor of Stamford Maritime Ltd; Mr Robert Cole, of Toplis and Harding, Loss Adjusters, and Mr Geoffrey Merton who gave me such good advice; Lloyd's of London, and, in particular, Mr Douglas Greenall, Head of Information; Mr David H. Larner, the Chief Press Officer, Information and Publicity Department, who so kindly helped me check the manuscript; Mr David Burling, Casualty Book Clerk, Intelligence Department, who gave me much of his valuable time; and Mr D. W. Presland, Deputy Head Waiter, for his help when dealing with enquiries.

The directors of La Societe Maritime Shell for granting me the privilege of visiting their magnificent ship, the ULCC, *Batillus*, her master, Commandant Alain Ruffloch, and his officers, for their courtesy and kindness; Monsieur J. Le Harivel, Relations Extérieures, for his invaluable help; and Commandant Edouard Lesimple and Monsieur Lucien Demain for the trouble they took on my behalf when they were so hard-pressed.

Dr Robin Tuckett, the best practical doctor I know, for sharing with me his invaluable experience in treating men suffering from 'the bends' — to which sphere of medicine he devoted much of his career.

Mr K. C. Scott for his kindness and invaluable technical advice.

Lastly, my gratitude is due to Mr Mervyn Temple-Richards, friend of a lifetime, who made this book possible.

All the characters in this book are fictitious but, if anyone should recognize him or herself, the fact is coincidental and I offer my apologies.

John Wingate
14 November 1977

LEVIATHAN

Preface to the Surveyor's Report

Too many innocent men's reputations have been at stake. Too many good men were being tainted by the smear of innuendo in the press. With the approval of the Committee, I have therefore deemed it right and proper to record, in fictional form, the events of those terrible days: memory fades, but the sinister aftermath will stay with us, a veritable Sword of Damocles, for generations.

I have naturally changed the names of the principal actors who briefly stepped across the world stage; if anyone who took part should identify himself, I, of course, offer my regrets and apologies. But if these unwilling participants should recognize themselves, perhaps they will condone my presumption — my sole purpose in publicly recording these events is to focus the light of truth upon the darkness which for too long has shrouded the incident which, to us in the Room, became known as the *Leviathan* affair.

J. K.

CHAPTER 1

'Okay, Dave, clear to vent...,' the controller in the mother-ship, *Guardian*, had ordered over the VHF.

David Krivine, pilot of the two-man submersible, *Seaveyor IV*, had nodded to his crew, Bert Strang, and down they had taken their mini-submarine to the murky seabed on the bottom of the North Sea. Whilst wallowing astern of the mother-ship, Strang had been sick. The boat smelt foul. Routine. Nothing abnormal in this, the last of their dives for this contract with Norlay.

At thirty-five, Krivine knew that his diving days were numbered. Already Norlay had dropped hints that he was needing a rest; so much had gone wrong during this difficult contract. Nerves were frayed by the constant breakdowns and appalling weather; the interminable delays caused by the hold-ups in supplies, seldom the fault of the supply vessels, had brought tempers to snarling-point at times; and, more frequently now, the big contractors were overtly backing up the government's pressure to use only divers and pilots who were not self-employed.

He was ranging in on the invisible oil pipe, guided by the controller, 270 feet above, when suddenly Bert Strang, the surveyor, who was also operating the lights, had alerted David to the rock face looming on their port bow in the swirling currents.

'Bring her to starboard, Dave,' Bert had warned. 'There's an overhang...'

Routine, even in this bloody North Sea where nothing went right... The last weld joint of the pipeline had been completed and checked; the supervising surveyor on the lay barge had checked the current, confirming it at 7.2 knots — and the depth, by the echo-sounder in the stern of the lay barge, as 286 feet. The joint had been pulled and, in spite of marginally adverse sea conditions, the skin-diver had managed to launch Bert and him, David Krivine, away on time. With surveying costs running at £12,000 a day, for this pipe lay to the new fields south of Brent, risks had to be taken if the survey was ever to be completed on time. *Seaveyor IV* was carrying out the last process in this difficult lay along the curved route which was only fifty feet wide; it ran across a nightmare maze of crevasses and underwater rock pinnacles — the blasting and the filling-in from the hopper barges had taken twice as long as estimated, because of bad weather that winter. But the nightmare was behind them now and Dave's job was to finish this last section of the 'as built' survey as rapidly as possible.

'Bloody hell — look, over there, Dave… Part of a section's suspended,' Bert had sung out. 'Can you ease her over a bit?'

Lying down and peering through his port, Dave made out a shadow in the cloud of muck swirling past in the fierce current. He increased power on his starboard motor, felt the tension mounting inside himself as he allowed *Seaveyor* to swing across the stream … he remembered realizing suddenly that power had failed on the port motor … the craft was swinging wildly to port, accentuated by extra revolutions from the starboard motor.

'Drive's gone on port,' he shouted at Strang.

Then everything went wild. In his tense state, he increased momentarily the starboard drive to 'full'. Before he could correct his error and throttle back, the furious current had swept the submersible downstream, to charge through the blackness.

'*Hold on...*' That had been his last order before she struck ... and the last words that Bert Strang was to register intelligibly for the rest of his days.

Seaveyor IV crashed hard against that underwater ledge. The shock flung David Krivine into the pilot's console, smashing his nose. The lights flicked out and from the darkness behind him he heard Bert call out. The submersible lunged into an almost vertical bow-down angle. David, thrust against the pilot's console, was unable to move while he waited for the craft to settle.

He wiped the warm blood from his face, tasted the salt. He began calling *Guardian*, when the dials and gauges surrounding him began gyrating crazily — and he knew no more.

When he regained his senses, his first action was to try and contact the mother-ship. He groped in the darkness, a twinge of panic pricking at him as he tried to orientate himself: *Seaveyor* was standing on her nose ... he must keep a hold of himself, calmly carry out the emergency drill he had exercised so often. First the power ... *where the devil was the main 120-volt breaker?*

He fumbled in the darkness, calling out again to Strang. The seats had come adrift and were wedged solid, separating each man from the other. As Dave's trembling fingers traced the dials and the air lines in the darkness, he felt suddenly the warmth of Strang's body. There was no reaction to his gentle prodding... David's hand slowly felt across the man's chest until it reached the face, then the head ... his fingers felt the warmth, the stickiness of congealing blood. The poor sod had cracked his skull upon some obtrusion: Strang was out to the wide. There was nothing to be done for Bert, until Dave could restore the power. Their survival depended on the main battery being intact; even if there was enough air, the CO_2 scrubbers could not be operated without juice — and the emergency battery would give them only eighteen hours ... then his fingers closed around the breaker, the largest on the switchboard. He paused an instant, tried to pray...

He heard the snap the breaker made — then the sphere was bathed in light. Strang was deathly pale; blood was oozing in a thick slime from a blue-black hole above his left temple. David tried to prop up the body, so that the head remained upright — but there was little more that he could do until he had carried out the emergency drill. His wristwatch still functioned: 23.19, 14 May. Any chance of rescue depended upon his accurate reporting to the mother-ship, 300 feet above them...

How much oxygen? How many amps? How long could power be supplied to the lithium hydroxide scrubbers which every half-hour reduced the increasing dose of carbon dioxide which would overcome them? He leaned across to read the gauges: first the two oxygen cylinders, then the battery readings and finally the HP air.

He tried to force his mind to work, to calculate the time remaining to them. If Strang died, the air would last twice as long ... and he thrust the abominable thought from his mind. But he could not concentrate, the figures vanishing from his thought processes as swiftly as he tried to solve the mental arithmetic. He found his pencil under the bench, jotted down the figures, tried to complete his communications log. With these figures swimming before his eyes, he flicked over the 'up' transducer switch: with *Seaveyor*'s vertical attitude, the 'up' transducer should be heard more clearly by *Guardian*. He could just detect a voice repeating, over and over again, '*Seaveyor, Seaveyor*, this is *Guardian*... Do you read me? *Over*...'

He tried to pull himself together, fought against the nausea swamping him — their lives depended upon an accurate technical report from him.

'This is *Seaveyor*, this is *Seaveyor*. I read you, loud and clear. Stand by my sitrep…'

The faint voice from the world above garbled through the loudspeaker on the console at his feet:

'Go ahead, Dave.'

He picked up the log, began reading the figures gyrating before his eyes. Gobs of blood spattered the paper … apathetically he wiped them off with the back of his hand, struggled to find the words… 'Strang unconscious, badly wounded in the head. *Seaveyor* standing on her nose. I think the ballast sphere has been holed when we struck this shelf. Current is pinning us here against a ledge. I'm okay but bleeding from damaged nose. Will call you every … will call…' He tried to think, tried to collect his thoughts. '…every…' His miniscule universe swam sickeningly, spinning, whirling… His head fell forwards, as he slumped across the battery of HP air cylinders.

CHAPTER 2

Jonathan Krivine bounded up the steps from the Bank underground station. Bill, the wrinkled humorist standing at the top, had little to say this morning as he shoved a damp *Financial Times* into Jonathan's hand.

'Partickerly nasty wevver, guv...' They grinned briefly at the well-worn messdeck joke (Bill had been shipmates with Jonathan's father during Hitler's war). Jonathan missed the significance of the cockney's further observations about his 'having served only in submarines and not in "X" craft', and hurried on his way.

The rain was slatting horizontally across Threadneedle Street and Jonathan bent double as he ran to the other side of the street, the curses of the taxi-drivers following him. This was the fifteenth of May: the cricket season; maypoles; voracious, gulping trout; the hay almost ready — wasn't that what May was supposed to be about? By the time he had reached Lime Street, his trousers from the knee downwards were clinging to his calves. He was thankful that he had chosen his number two suit this morning — the insatiable demands of the tax-man, the expenses of their newly-acquired house on the Isle of Sheppey and the children's ever-demanding needs, made the cost of a good suit something he could no longer afford. He reached the main entrance to Lloyd's and stood for a moment, shaking off the wet and regaining his breath.

The doorman with the welcoming smile and the waiters of Lloyd's — these servants were the backbone of this vast corporation: it was they, and the devoted clerks, who kept the wheels turning, in spite of the computers which were now rendering bearable the burden of paperwork. He descended to the cloakroom, dried himself off, and checked in the mirror that he was presentable.

True, his beard was beginning to show the odd grey hair, but, at thirty-five, it was a man's beard, a virile, sailor's face-fungus, black, with blond patches about the lower jaw. A trustworthy face, he decided, though the brown eyes were showing signs of secretiveness, of suspicion; but when he smiled (which he deliberately tried in front of the looking-glass) the dry humour with which he was supposed to be blessed, broke through the severity of the ex-naval officer's face. As the attendant brushed the back of his coat, the doubts assailed him once again. Had he made the right decision to leave the navy, to resign his short-service commission? Too late now to cry over the past; his new life at Lloyd's was interesting, more exciting, perhaps, than the life of a peace-time officer in a service at the mercy of volatile politicians.

'Thanks. Foul day, Jim,' and he smiled at the attendant who was reputed to know the name of every member of Lloyd's. Jonathan Krivine hurried up the marble stairway and collected his copy of Lloyd's List and Lloyd's Shipping Index. He passed the entrance to the Nelson Room (revered by his father) with its magnificent collection of silver plate and the log book of HMS *Euryalus* wherein was recorded Nelson's famous signal; and then he crossed to the central bay at the end of the gallery overlooking 'the Room'. He paused here every day to collect his thoughts before starting the day's work in his 'box'. Contemplating the scene in the Room below him was an exercise which helped him; the daily irritants were reduced to size if he could spare a few moments for thought before the hectic day started. And this morning he had arranged to meet Jeremy Pedrick here on the gallery; he was a broker of his own age, from Sturgess, Hardy and Boldre, one of the lesser-known firms. An interesting enquiry had just come in…

This new building was a magnificent edifice. Fully equipped to serve its members (nearly 9,000 now), the Room below him swept, crescent-shaped, into the distance 340 feet away. The Room, the centre of the world's insurance underwriting, was larger in area than that of the average city block — and yet it was never spacious enough to house all its members, its staff and the ancillary services. Here, at the heart of the world's insurance business, underwriter and broker met to conduct their business.

The broker represented the ship-owner who wished to insure his ship and his cargo; the broker understood what the owner wanted, knew intimately the ship's state, the quality of her officers and crew, how and with what cargo she was loaded. On the frank information which the broker supplied, the Lloyd's underwriter could assess the risk and thus price his premium. Broker and underwriter were bound to have confidence in each other; their business was contracted upon total trust — an underwriter would honour a claim, once he had initialled the line on the broker's 'slip' and even before the legal contract had been produced by the Policy Signing Office. 'Fidentia' the motto of Lloyd's, could not have been chosen more aptly for this colossus. Yes, he had made the right decision. He was proud to be a name in Joe Lethbridge's syndicate, Lethbridge and Seymour; one of the best, but not one of the largest, at Lloyd's.

The Room was beginning to fill up below him. The dark blue and crimson liveried 'waiters' (so-called from the turbulent days of 1688, when marine risks were placed in the hurly-burly of Lloyd's Coffee House) were already going about their business; the Caller was checking his microphone and communication systems in the rostrum beneath the Lutine bell; and the 'boxes', the overcrowded pens which stretched in three banks down the length of the Room, were already filling up. He could just distinguish Joe Lethbridge, his leading underwriter, who accepted the risks on behalf of all the names in the syndicate. The mass of files and indexes in each box had at first bewildered Jonathan but, after three years, he was already beginning to profit by his short experience. He got on well with Joe, a wise old bird, who was handing over more responsibility to Jonathan as the years slipped by. Joe had worked for years with Jonathan's father, Jocelyn Krivine, who had retired two years ago. Joe had learnt much from him, which was one reason why Jonathan now found himself a name in Lethbridge's syndicate.

The younger Krivine glanced at his watch: Jeremy Pedrick was seldom late — probably a hitch over a broker's slip he might be bringing along this morning. There were rumours flying around the market that an unidentified giant was about to place considerable business at Lloyd's — but, so far, the rumours had remained gossip. The usual gathering was clustered about the casualty reports and the latest news which were prepared by the Intelligence Department and displayed on the noticeboards opposite the rostrum. Jonathan would bring himself up-to-date on the way to his box, after he had finished with Jeremy.

His clothes were beginning to dry. He did not object to discomfort as much as some of his city colleagues — his few years in the navy had taught him that. He wondered what his father, now reaching old age, really thought about his twin brother, David's, decisions. The old man had advised against their departure from the Royal Navy, but he had never blamed them. After Healey's suicidal cuts in '77, who could say that David had done the wrong thing?

He, Jonathan, had always been the more careful, the less intrepid of the twins — he had always accepted that. Perhaps he had taken after his father, while David had inherited the spontaneity and exuberance of their mother? Or perhaps Jonathan was the more stable, because he was legally the senior of the two twins: their births had been separated by only twenty minutes. From their earliest days, David had suffered the demon of jealousy, unconsciously being driven to outdo his brother. So close had they been to each other that they read each other's minds and understood each other too well as they grew older. David always had to be first across the line, jump further, win the cycle race, climb the highest tree ... poor old Dad, he had endured difficult years bringing up his twin sons, after their mother's death when they were five.

Father had inherited the imperturbability of their grandfather, the forebear who had made the Krivines. Francisk Krivine was a Lithuanian Jew, born in Memel in 1901. A young man during the Bolshevik revolution, he had taken his father's advice and slipped across to Poland where he began as an apprentice in a Danzig timber firm.

By 1933, Francisk Krivine had saved enough to start his own business; two years later, his firm had progressed sufficiently for him to become an exporter of Baltic timber; it was during one of his visits to Hull that he grew attached to the tolerant way of life of the British. He made contacts and prudently began to shift his capital to Yorkshire. When Hitler exploited the 'Danzig corridor' as a pretext for his forthcoming invasion of Poland, the decisive and impetuous Francisk decided that this was the moment to quit. He left Danzig secretly one night, taking with him his wife and son, now sixteen. He sent his son to Ampleforth so that he and his wife could devote their entire energies to the creation of a timber business on the banks of the Humber. In 1937, he applied for British naturalization, but kept his Polish citizenship. He changed his son's Christian name to Jocelyn, after the Yorkshireman who had helped him immigrate.

When the Nazi horde slaughtered Poland, Francisk applied to join the Polish Army in Britain, but he was turned down because of the heart trouble he had developed. Instead, MI5 used him as a static agent, an expert on the information filtering from the Baltic States. He thus was able to continue managing his timber business at Hull, while Jocelyn finished his last school year. The son was nineteen when he joined the Royal Navy in the spring of 1940 as an ordinary seaman, RNVR. The youth's ability soon gained him a commission and he ended his war as first lieutenant of a fleet destroyer in the Far East.

There was little left of his father's business, when Lieutenant Jocelyn Krivine left the navy to re-start his life. The timber business firm had been burnt to cinders by Goering's Luftwaffe. But Grandfather Francisk's old Yorkshire friend had contacts in the City and Jocelyn began his new life as a broker, under-studying in Turk, Smith and Prentice, one of Lloyd's brokers in Mincing Lane. He married his adorable actress wife as soon as he was secure; two years later his twin sons were born.

Perhaps, thought Jonathan, as he gazed down upon the thickening crowd in the Room, the death of their mother had provided his father with the motivation to struggle his utmost for his two offspring. Whatever the mainspring, Jocelyn Krivine had ended up as senior partner in Turk, Smith and Prentice ten years before he retired. He had been pleased that his son, Jonathan, had accepted the chance which had been presented to him by Jocelyn's greatest friend in the navy, Joe Lethbridge. But Dad talked seldom, and never with either brother about his hopes or disappointments. What were the old man's secret reactions to David's tempestuous life, Jonathan wondered?

Then he spotted Jeremy Pedrick down in the Room, peering at the day's news on the Intelligence noticeboards. Jonathan raised his hand, but Jeremy turned his face towards the Caller. What was keeping Jeremy? The frigid reception of Jonathan's greeting was out of character.

Dear old Dave — what was he up to now? That broken marriage with Christine ... what a disaster but, as usual, Dave had ignored both Dad's and his, Jonathan's, advice. At the moment, David was embroiled with the Inland Revenue over his 'self-employed' status. He was as obstinate as he was generous, being unable to accept that he could not win against the State octopus. The government were insisting that all North Sea divers had to be subject to normal pay-as-you-earn deductions. Their obnoxious inference was that all self-employed were dishonest. They were perhaps justified in some cases, but a diver was, literally, in a world of his own. It was bloody dangerous down at 300-feet-plus, in the icy waters of the North Sea. Men of that breed could not be compelled to become civil servants.

But Dave had a chip on his shoulder — no doubt about it. Looking back on it all, his attitude sprang from their youth and the spontaneity he had inherited from their unremembered mother. Dave acted first, thought afterwards — an example being his foolhardiness when, on the Sunday before their camping holiday in Scotland, Dad had taken them up to Ilkley Moor for a picnic. Dad was snoozing in the heather, while his two impossible twins were climbing the Scotch firs behind him. Jonathan, who was the taller of the two at this stage of their development, dared David to swing across to another branch on an adjacent fir, as he, Jonathan, had just successfully achieved. Dave misjudged his swing and, in his haste, fell, breaking his wrist. So their holiday had been delayed a day, and the rest of it spoilt by Dave's gloating inability to help with the washing-up because of his plastered hand.

Jonathan grinned to himself — precious memories, but he wished that his father could have found someone with whom to share his last days — he should have married again. He had found joy through his sons, though they were vastly different. At times, Jonathan found it difficult not to feel smug. He knew he was reliable, hard-working and making a success of things for Margaret and the kids. His city life absorbed his working week, but her life was fulfilled with their six year old, Alastair, and Katie, aged five. Jonathan was more British than the British now, choosing the right names for their offspring in deference to Margaret's Scottish parents. The Danzig background and their Jewish antecedents seemed far distant, after he had adopted the Catholic faith at Ampleforth. His daydreaming was interrupted by the sight of Jeremy Pedrick striding across the end of the gallery towards him. Jonathan glanced at his watch.

'Sorry to keep you, Jonathan. My cattle truck was held up outside Wimbledon for over half an hour.' He was glancing curiously at Jonathan. 'I stopped at the Information Board to check on the news.'

'I saw you from here.'

'I wanted to be certain. I only heard it on the eight o'clock.' Jeremy was frowning and glancing sideways at the Lloyd's underwriter. 'There's nothing in the stop press. It happened some time about midnight, so the teleprinter reports.'

Jonathan felt an irritation smouldering inside him.

'What are you trying to tell me, Jeremy?'

'Did you underwrite Norlay — the North Sea surveying outfit?' Jeremy asked quietly.

'No. My brother David is one of their submersible pilots. I'm superstitious.' But he sensed it, the touch of impending disaster...

Jeremy touched his sleeve: 'His submarine's in trouble, Jonathan, stuck at 300 feet. His crew is hurt and the rescuers are having trouble communicating with David.'

So that was it — and Jonathan began threading his way towards the telephones.

'How long's he got, Jeremy?' he asked curtly over his shoulder.

'The news was uncommittal. The final lifting attempt began at first light this morning.'

CHAPTER 3

The wind was starting to buffet *Guardian*'s superstructure. Tom Tregannion, controller of submersible operations, offered a silent prayer that the miraculous break in the weather would hold for one more hour. The barometer was falling again and the clouds lowering to masthead height, as the mother-ship rolled to her anchors in this thick night. Just another hour — and he moved apart from the group of orange, oil-skinned men who were clustered around the hoist, all of them mesmerized by the 3½-inch polypropylene rope that was plucking *Seaveyor IV* from the bed of the North Sea.

'Watch out for the nylon line,' shouted the surface officer. 'Don't let it foul…' Tregannion succeeded in chewing back his blistering reproach. After two sleepless days and nights, and with intermittent food, nerves were strung taut.

Guardian was wallowing gently in the swell. Thank God she was not pitching — the recovery rope was designed to stand the snatch if it had to, even if *Guardian* pitched, but the strain would have been immense.

The working-lights were throwing pools of light across the gleaming deck. Two cables to starboard, *Callender*'s lights danced across the horizon. She had steamed at full speed from Aberdeen with her emergency kit of diving gear and a team of saturation divers. She had arrived on the scene at 23.15, yesterday, 15 May and it was her efficient help which had finally triumphed in this battle against time and the weather.

He had worked too rapidly, Tregannion realized now. He should have waited for *Callender*, but at least *Guardian*'s available diver had been able to give an exact report on

Seaveyor's position and her orientation. He had been a courageous man — and resourceful — for it was he who suggested establishing two snatch blocks on the rocky seabed. With these, by reeving hauling-off wires, the trapped submersible could be hauled from beneath the ledge.

The first attempt had failed because one of the holdfasts had shifted. The final attempt had proceeded without a hitch. God willing, in a few moments *Seaveyor* should break surface...

'Thirty feet, sir,' the surface officer was shouting.

Guardian's searchlights were playing on the sea astern, a rippling, mercurial surface, on which three Geminis were milling like water beetles.

'*Slow!*' The winch operator nodded and the whine of the hoist motors decreased.

Tregannion walked aft, stood by the rail beneath the lifting gantry. Though the divers had followed the submersible all the way since she had cleared the shelf, no one had yet been in contact with Dave Krivine since his last intelligible report at 00.45 this morning, 16 May — forty-nine hours since the start of the emergency. Since 00.45 — silence. Tom Tregannion was not looking forward to the next few minutes. Krivine had already reported that Strang was probably dying from a head injury.

There was a shout from one of the Geminis. The surface bulged; the lifting toggle broke surface. In silence, the extra safety strops were passed, the towing line secured. *Seaveyor*, tons heavy now, could still slip from their grasp at this last second... Tregannion held his breath as a diver raised his hand in acknowledgment to the surface officer's order. He saw the man's head probing into the blister of the upper hatch...

The first body to be lifted out was Bert Strang's: it was too slight to be David's. His arms hung limply downwards and he seemed ridiculously small in the grasp of the three divers manhandling him gently into the Gemini. There was still no report from them over the R/T ... then Tom felt the doc standing by his side. No use asking bloody silly questions at this moment ... and then the other diver went down for Krivine.

It was an eternity before they extricated the large bulk from the hatch. Still nothing from the R/T — *he must be dead*. What the hell were they waiting for? The head was hanging down but they were waiting for something ... and then Tregannion saw the massive chest heaving, the enormous blond head wagging suddenly as Krivine vomited across the lip of the hatch coaming.

A cheer rang out from *Guardian*'s working deck. A Gemini's R/T crackled: 'Dave's okay...'

Tom Tregannion felt a lump in his throat, as the doc put an arm about his shoulder.

Tregannion felt very tired. He was sitting by the sickbay bunk in which the doc had insisted Dave should be temporarily constricted, until he was fit enough to be transferred to *Callender*.

The rescue ship was to take Strang, Krivine, and the doctor to the nearest production platform whence a helicopter waited to whisk them to the Faeroes for onward flight to Aberdeen.

The doc had flushed Dave through with oxygen and, in those few minutes before he flopped into this bottomless sleep, the man who had returned from the dead managed to etch in the sequence of events during those forty-nine hours, twenty minutes. The CO_2 scrubbers had failed after the second afternoon, probably due to malfunction from the battery power somewhere in the circuits. Dave had managed to continue with his routine reports, in spite of worsening headaches as the CO_2 poisoning built up. The pain had grown unbearable, but he had remained conscious, flushing pure oxygen into the sphere. He could recall little of the last few hours: his one obsession was that he had been unable to do more for Bert.

Tregannion would remember for the rest of his days the lifting of the cloud from Krivine's face when the doc told him that Strang was alive and would reach hospital safely. Then, after a local anaesthetic, Dave's smashed nose was cleaned up and plastered, ready for the surgeons. The exhausted pilot then slumped into sleep.

'Let him be, Tom. He won't wake for hours yet.' The doc was scrubbing his hands in the sink.

'Thanks,' Tom said. 'I'll stay for a bit. It's a cruel day for Dave.'

The doctor shook his head, not comprehending. He shut the sickbay door quietly behind him.

Tregannion glanced again at the large man in the bunk. Dave was a good guy and a good diver. His sense of fun made him popular wherever he was. His heavy face, in spite of the gory plasters, was grey but the man's shaggy head, even in sleep, was set proudly on that deep-barrelled chest which was the hallmark of so many divers. His hands, scarred and battered from years of underwater work on the platforms and pipelines, lay like a child's across the stained sheet. Hands like hams, with immense strength in those fingers, they said. One of the best divers in the business, if he had been more temperamentally stable. His temper was notorious, once he was roused; more than once Tom had had to grovel to the police, when Dave had hit the whisky after a gruelling spell on the surveys. But that had been before David met that woman whom Tom had once come across in the MFV which provided a catering service for the supply vessels: Sally, full of character, just the girl for Dave, might settle him down. He would be needing her now, after Dave realized the implications of the injury he had suffered.

The doc had whispered quietly to Tom that the nose damage had probably put an end to any further top-grade diving for David Krivine. But only Tregannion knew that Norlay had already decided that this was to be Krivine's last contract with them. His self-employed status and his age were much against him, while these fresh, highly-trained youngsters were coming forward for employment.

'Thank God you're safe, Dave,' Tom whispered to himself. 'And thank God, too, I don't have to tell you now why they're sacking you.'

David's Cortina should be swinging round the bend in the lane at any moment. He had said six o'clock, but nothing was certain with these late appointments at the hospital...

Sally Grant was a realist. She had to be, she realized, as she slipped off her gloves and straightened her back from weeding the rockery which was their pride and joy now that David had time on his hands during his convalescence. While she was down at the MFV, during those first weeks after the *Seaveyor* accident, David was content to remain here, in the garden of Ling Croft which they had bought jointly. She had no illusions about this man; he was a complex, unpredictable character. She adored him.

Sally Grant stood for a moment, peering at the Sma' Glen, the shallow valley between the hills running towards Carn Mor; the mountain stood gaunt and black against the sweeping clouds this evening. Already, there were patches of purple amongst the boulders — the first ling was beginning to caress this beautiful country with its colour and scent. It was there, in the Glen, that they had first kissed.

Life would never be the same again for either of them now. They had come too far to retract. She did not regret for a moment their new-found happiness together. She turned her back on the Sma' Glen, hurried through the blue of the Jackmanii clematis entwining the porch of their cottage. She could watch the lane while she rustled up supper.

She was glad she was two years younger than David. His ego needed the age difference — he had suffered too many knocks recently. His disguised dismissal by Norlay, when they declined to renew his contract for the next pipe-lay, had hurt him badly. But that disappointment had been before this second operation to his sinuses, when there had been a chance of repairing the damage. This evening she would know the surgeon's final verdict. This was David's Rubicon: she had hated seeing him hurt during these past weeks, while he tried to sell himself for further submersible contracts.

She could hear their tree pipit 'tchk-tchking' outside the window. She stopped scraping the carrots to flick it the breadcrumbs which she kept in a saucer. David loved this perfection of creation. 'Pipit' was his second pleasant duty, after he had shouldered his frame through their tiny porch. She smiled to herself — what a strange mixture of strength and gentleness was her man ... the little bird pranced cautiously towards the crumbs, its head cocked, its bright eye wary. The beak flicked — the crumbs were gone, as he hopped out of range to finish the delicacy.

She wished that David would stop blaming himself for Bert Strang's tragic condition: there was little hope for him now, they said. His damaged brain would leave him a vegetable for life, unable to speak, to think or to care for himself for the remainder of his days. In her arms, shortly after the accident, he had confessed to her his momentary lapse at the controls of that submersible. He blamed the craft's accident on his incompetency, but he had told no one. 'There's no point in committing suicide myself, is there?' he had asked in the darkness, whilst they listened to the chuckle of the stream tumbling through its peaty bed at the bottom of the garden.

So he had tried to persuade some of his friends to form a company of trained divers. Only one had the guts to say that he was scared of the new legislation — being a 'self-employed' diver was a dangerous game these days, in more senses than one. He had come home to her, overwhelmed by a black despair which she prayed she would never have to assuage again; in their loving, she had brought him back to the rational world. It was then he had learnt from Tom Tregannion that a one-man-band underwater, anti-fouling business in Falmouth was going bankrupt.

She had encouraged him to chase the opportunity — at least he could surmount his depression, whilst there was something to aim for... She had taken three days off from her precious business, Catering Services (Offshore) Ltd, and together they had inspected the failed enterprise in Falmouth. He could make a success of it, he was sure; he had already designed an anti-fouling 'crawler'. Anti-fouling modern VLCCs would require diving up to seventy-foot depths (perhaps later, when the ULCCs arrived, up to ninety feet) and the surgeon had assured him that his nasal passages would be able to stand these pressures. So they had stopped off a night in London to see his brother, Jonathan. The twin had been sympathetic but had gently declined to put up the £3,000 deposit required by the Falmouth bank manager for a £12,000 loan. The defunct business was offered at £5,000 which included twenty yards of waterfront, sufficient for David's 'crawlers' which he had so often dreamed about.

Sally had met Jonathan after the meeting. She was not sure about him, but she could understand his smugness and disapproval. This was not the first time David had asked for help, nor was Sally his first 'wife'. She was sure that Jonathan had been genuine when he had stated that he was fully extended himself: an interesting enquiry might be coming his way and his underwriting required every penny he could raise. Why didn't David slip down to Bromley and ask Dad if he could help? They had telephoned Jocelyn Krivine from Jonathan's office and travelled at once to the old man's home.

Sally glanced up from the worktop and looked out at the glen. The love of a father for his son was a rare thing these days. She could understand David better, now that she had met the father. A kind man, he had been gentle with her; she would never forget his silent benediction, as he had slowly walked with them to the station. He would do what he could to help; he would have a word with the Falmouth bank.

That had been six days ago. The bank would give their decision within a month: loans were difficult these days. She heard the scrunching of tyres on the unmetalled lane. She slipped the pinafore from her waist, fluffed up her black hair in the mirror above the sink and ran to the gate leading to the lean-to garage.

He lay on his back, her head tucked into the crook of his shoulder. The moon had woken him. He felt her stir as he turned to read the time by the old clock ticking by their bedside: twelve minutes past two in the morning. She muttered something in her sleep and clung closely to him.

The moon was full, a golden dish suspended unnaturally in the indigo heavens. For a few more minutes it would hang above the Sma' Glen, bathing the hills with its cold light; it would set behind the Cairngorms and Carn Mor. A precious moment this, with Sally in his arms, stretched beside him. He tightened his arm about her, heard her sigh of content. Her short black hair was tickling his nostril as he stroked her cheek. She slipped away from his arms, waiting for him in the moonlight.

What had he done to deserve such a woman? She was so small but, God, what character lay behind that elusively ordinary face. At thirty-three she was the right age for him, but her face, already lined by the vicissitudes of her life, breathed character, from her broad forehead beneath the jet-black hair, down to her puckish chin. Her features were in repose at this moment, a faint smile at the corners of her wide mouth with its red, red lips. It was her eyes that had conquered him: green pools, touched by restless golden-brown flecks, like the lights flickering in a moorland brook. She was a bundle of restless energy, ever inquisitive, always seeking fresh delight from the world. It was no accident that she was making a success of her catering business.

Ronald and she had married with little thought of the morrow. When he had been declared redundant he had launched the catering business from the MFV in Aberdeen's inner harbour. Living on board and using the boat as the office, the business took off like a rocket — with few overheads, Ronald was able to undercut most of his competitors and soon the cash was flowing in. But his disorganization and congenital urge to beat the tax-man had reaped disaster when the inevitable auditors had moved in ... and that was when he had disappeared, taking all the ready cash. Sally had heard from him once; he had told her that he was living with a woman from the south and would not be coming back.

Sally had picked herself up, refusing to indulge in self-pity; she immediately tackled the multitude of problems that swamped her. She had a way with the skippers of the supply boats and the administrators managing the platforms and the ancillary services; she realized, too, that there was little wrong with the business which needed only a determined, methodical approach to put it back on its feet. Within six months, Catering Services (Offshore) Ltd was in the black again. Ronald would not resign his directorship; he had quickly realized there was potential in the company, after all. He refused to sign the accounts when Sally asked for a divorce.

Then David had met her one Sunday down in the harbour. An April shower had caught her at the far end of the quay, the rain slashing across the harbour and spattering the cobbles. She had no raincoat and was trying to reach the bus shelter. He had slowed the Cortina and pushed open the door for her. Backing against the squall, she had hopped in beside him, her hair like rat's tails, her face shining from the wet.

'You're soaked,' he said, leaning across to slam the door. The little woman seemed helpless, as she struggled to squeeze her two briefcases on the floor.

'Bugger this rain,' she snapped. 'It's not me I'm worried about — it's my files.' She stabbed the briefcase with her tiny shoe.

Even he had been shocked. She had looked up at him, angry as hell. 'My annual accounts...'

He had tried to suppress his amusement — and then, slowly, she had begun to chuckle. They laughed together ridiculously and, in the strange silence which followed, he looked into her eyes — and that had been that. He had known many women, but this was real … something splendid and precious, not to be sullied or spoiled. He had dropped her off at her lodgings…

The moon had slid behind the rowan tree. Dappled shadows were creeping along the wall behind their headboard, advancing towards the sheets. And as his eyes savoured again the form spread by his side, he felt the touch of her hand.

'David,' she said softly. 'No — not yet. I've been thinking while you've been at the hospital. Put your head here — while I talk.'

And in the dappled moonlight, she talked while she stroked his head.

'I saw the solicitor today. It's five years.'

'He's wrong.'

'No. Ron refuses to budge. He wants to stay in CSO.'

'We'll buy him out,' David said.

'What with, my dear? You're not earning yet.' She said it kindly, not meaning to hurt.

'Five years, then — you'll be thirty-eight.'

'He would never give me the child I wanted.' She pulled him closer and he felt her softness.

'You'll be nearly thirty-nine,' he said, 'before you can have my son.'

'Not necessarily, David.' She kissed him on the forehead. 'I've thought it all out — all the relative values. I know what I want, what's right. But it depends on you, whether you think it right for our child.'

'What do you mean?'

'I love you, David — I love you, perhaps more, even, than you love me. Never forget that.'

He closed his arm about her, cradling her tiny body.

'I want our son ... yours,' she whispered. 'I want my little David. I can't afford to wait.' An owl was screeching up in the glen.

'Now. This morning. In this moonlight.'

And, later, she crept into his encircling arms. He could feel her heart beating, as sleep claimed them both.

'I forgot,' she whispered. 'There's an advert in the *Evening News* — just the thing for you, while you're waiting for the bank's decision.'

'Not now,' he murmured. 'In the morning.'

He heard her murmuring next to him; remembered first light stealing behind the outline of the hills; registered that the stars were fading one by one. And then he fell asleep.

CHAPTER 4

The ex-Princess from Singaradja did not use her title. Princess Usha, from one of the most noble families in Bali, was now the wife of one of the world's richest men — and she glanced with faint amusement at the coarse little man sprawling in the chair which he had pushed back from the dining table. A Havana smouldered from between his stubby fingers as, dressed in his favourite dinner jacket, he savoured to the full his rare display of gracious living. He had invited his operations manager to dine at Triton Place, this beautiful Hertfordshire estate which he had bought four years ago.

'I'm sure Mr Carlsen would like another glass of port,' she reminded her husband tactfully. 'You're talking so much about your precious ships, Kartar. You've forgotten your guest.'

Kartar Alexander Browne ignored her, swept the cut-glass decanter, its ruby richness glinting from the candlelight, towards the clever Dane who was hired to execute his orders.

'No, thanks, sir. I've a long drive in front of me.' He glanced from beneath his lids at his hostess. 'A magnificent dinner, Mrs Browne.'

Usha smiled. Knud Carlsen was no fool; the only man whom Kartar paid generously, he was probably the closest person in the world to her husband — but a friend — no. Kartar had no friends. 'I travel alone,' he often reminded her. 'It's quicker that way. I don't object to trampling on people if they're strangers.'

She snipped off another sprig of grapes with the silver George III scissors. She contemplated the two men on either side of her; it was difficult to believe that Kartar owned and controlled his vast octopus, Planeka Shipping International, whose marine tentacles were tending to set world rates, to the irritation of the established companies. An acquaintance had said of Kartar, 'Boy! If he can undercut the Greeks and still stay in the shipping game, he must be smart — and tough.'

Her husband was a strange mixture: ambitious and ruthless, yet he admired the British and their unique system to the point of absurdity; he was more English than the English, but how long his Anglophilism would survive after the Americans had helped him so sumptuously with the building of *Leviathan* and *Goliath* — and when the Inland Revenue finally nobbled him — remained to be seen. The English gentleman's hypocritical contempt for filthy lucre was something alien; Kartar had difficulty in concealing his lust for the power which real wealth gave him — but that was un-British too. He was trying to conquer this failing and relied on Usha to correct him when his lack of breeding showed.

She had remonstrated with her husband about his purchase of Triton Place. She hated it, disliked the flat, uninteresting countryside and the dormitory community. She had taken charge of the redecoration of the old house: her restrained taste had transformed it into one of the loveliest estates in the kingdom. She had not forgotten the day when the Brownes seemed to have reached the summit of the social scale: *Country Life* wanted an article on Triton Place. It had been amusing, watching him wrestling with his schizophrenic desires: her Kartar was not often mixed up. His obsession was to accumulate wealth for the power it gave him. He had certainly succeeded, but he had left a trail of broken lives behind him, those whom he had used, then discarded once he had achieved his ambition.

The two men were talking oil politics. She would have to endure the tedium a little longer. Kartar had met someone who would discreetly give as good as he got: Knud was a good listener — difficult to trample him.

Kartar's extraordinary character, she was convinced, stemmed from his mixed blood. The union of his planter father (a Harrovian who had left his homeland under doubtful circumstances) with the daughter of a Javanese shipping magnate, had resulted in the birth in Semerang of their only son. Singapore had surrendered; the invincible Japanese were poised to leap into Sumatra, when General Alexander had calmly extricated the demoralized British Army from Burma and arrested the yellow horde at the gate of India. Mr Browne and his intelligent and beautiful wife decided to move out.

Hastily naming their offspring after his father-in-law and the British general, the Brownes quit Java in the last ship to sail for Africa. They took all their capital with them, wrapped about his wife's body, and settled in Dar-es-Salaam. With their combined astuteness, Mr Browne soon worked up the remains of his father-in-law's Javanese shipping firm into a thriving coastal trade.

The war by-passed them, but not the profits. When the young son was old enough, he was sent to the leading prep school in Salisbury, whence he was despatched to Harrow for the English education which Browne had always desired for his progeny.

Kartar Alexander Browne, an exceptionally intelligent and industrious youth, applied himself to his studies and won the top Cambridge scholarship. While his contemporaries savoured the pleasures of cricket and the Cam, the strange, self-effacing undergraduate with the smouldering black eyes bent over his books in the dank room of his lodgings. Perhaps it was this self-imposed exclusion which had influenced him so forcibly — but, from those days onwards, even after his first-class degree, Kartar Alexander Browne deliberately built up an impenetrable stockade about himself.

Kartar had no wish to return to the steamy tropics, but his father inconveniently died from alcoholic poisoning, leaving the shipping business to his son. Joining his mother in Dar-es-Salaam, Kartar Browne decided within the month that the hurricane of change was blowing too hotly throughout the African continent. Secretly he began to manipulate his affairs, to create the future structure of the international shipping company about which he dreamed. Using the assets from the discreet sales of the East African shipping firm, he quietly slipped out of Africa and set up Planeka Shipping International, its registered office being in a semi-detached Victorian villa in the East End.

His self-imposed and lonely barrier had paid off; as he often reminded his wife, 'I manage my own affairs. Why should I pay advisers to tell me what I have already decided to do?' He worked alone and was usually two jumps ahead of his competitors. When Kartar had made up his mind, he would allow no one, nothing, to deflect him from his objective.

He had bought Triton Place for two reasons: one, for the sense of achievement; two, for the seclusion the estate gave him. He had erected an electric fence around the property and employed a security firm to ensure privacy. He was ignored by 'The County', despised by the locals. He had no hobbies, but had installed an aviary for the breeding of pheasants, exotic birds and peacocks, the latter roaming the gardens and wrecking them. The beauty of the birds was his only pleasure. He would allow no shooting of the pheasants: the fence effectively deterred the poachers.

In a moment of aberration, Usha had given him an electric organ, hoping that the instrument which he played with such talent might deflect his mind from his only natural hobby — that of making money. But she had been relieved when finally he had given up the music — the booming of the organ inspired a maniacal atmosphere as it resonated through the empty house — *Jane Eyre* and *Wuthering Heights* rolled into one...

Kartar was sipping the iced water which he always drank — he never touched alcohol, whether because of his inborn Islamic traditions or because of his health, she had never been able to find out. Physical exercise was a fetish of his, but it was his only indulgence. He had bought a gymnasium, a pool and a sauna. He had never yet invited anyone to share these luxuries and had forbidden her to invite the small circle of acquaintances which she had made during these four years. No invitations reached Triton Place now. The mysterious foreigners at the Big House were left to themselves. Kartar Browne had achieved, once again, what he wanted.

Usha stifled her sigh of frustration. At forty-two, he was four years older than her ... and as she watched him beneath her unpainted lids, she had to admit that he was still a fit man: stocky, with powerful shoulders, he showed no stomach as did so many of his British contemporaries. He affected a British military moustache and strutted like one of his peacocks, but, beneath his sallow skin, she had never seen the flush of anger. Only his eyes ever showed emotion. Kartar was the most controlled, ice-cold man she had ever had the misfortune to meet.

She had just surfaced after a disastrous affair with the son of a Baroda potentate, when her father had sent her on a safari holiday where she had met Kartar in Dar-es-Salaam. He had already begun to realize his fortune, but a beautiful and cultured wife was what he coveted most. In her innocence and raw state she had truly believed that he loved her — poor Kartar, he could never know the meaning of the word. He loved himself too much. He had bought her, she had soon realized, as he bought everything else.

'Kartar, I'll ask Deirdre to bring the coffee into the drawing-room when you're ready. A brandy, Mr Carlsen?' She rose from the table. 'No? You'll excuse me, but I must telephone my mother in Negara — you know what age is. She expects the call every month. It's one of her joys.'

As she glided from the room, her silk sari whispering about her, she knew that both men's eyes were upon her. She was tall, nearly five foot eleven, and she moved with the stealth and grace of a tigress. She enjoyed admiration and after closing the dining-room door behind her, she stood before the gilt-framed mirror above the marble mantelpiece.

Thirty-eight ... the serene, golden face of the Bali woman was as aloof and dignified as ever, but her placid mouth had developed twists of bitterness at the corners. Wealth, position, power brought less happiness than the unselfishness of a village washer-woman with her teeming children. She suffered black despair, tortured moments when she was utterly alone, when she sighed for the tumbling crystal of the streams through the tropical vegetation; the vivid colours of the volcanic hills behind the forest. She had visited her family only once, but never again ... the wrench of leaving them had torn her apart. Her people, warm people, with a zest for loving and living — she missed them with a passion her husband could never understand. If only he could have been a normal man, with the healthy appetites she craved, how happy their marriage could have been. Instead — childless, passionless, a dead existence.

'My God,' she whispered. 'Is that you, Usha, staring from the mirror? You, the child with high hopes, bare-footed amongst the wild flowers of the hills?' She turned suddenly from the mask, the flat, dead eyes peering at her accusingly, the brown, listless eyes that were once alive with hope: a ghoul's face, lined by frustration, buttoned like a glove.

She pressed the bell and waited for Deirdre's blue-and-white, trim figure to bustle through the door. The maid was the only true friend Usha had.

'We should have fought the nuclear-power lobby with everything the oil world possessed,' Knud Carlsen said, relighting his cigar. He had better watch his step: Kartar Browne could not take criticism — but to hell with it, they had dined well and there were few moments when he and the chairman could really speak their minds. Kartar was a unique one — apart from using his operations manager for the detailed running of Planeka, that human dynamo across the table, a wizard at finance in the shipping business, did all the thinking himself. He had started a remarkably short time ago with his first 2,000-ton coastal tanker: now Planeka Shipping International was influencing global bulk-carrier prices.

'An idiotic remark of yours, Knud, if you will forgive me. How could we have known in the late seventies, when the French went nuclear because they had no oil, that the EEC would produce ZETA half a century ahead of time? Now that nuclear power can be transformed directly into electrical energy, who the hell wants to buy oil, to heat boilers, to make steam to drive bloody turbines? That's at the root of the trouble…' and he slapped the gleaming mahogany with the palm of his hand so that the glasses rang.

In the silence, Knud watched the genius across the table pondering the economic problems; a crude-carrying company needed a fortune-teller on its board these days. After two years with Kartar Browne, Carlsen had learned how to work with him: never cross him, let him have his way on the things that mattered. The operations manager could take care of the running of the fleet — but God help him if anything went wrong: the tin-tack, there and then. Kartar Browne had reached the summit the hard way; he understood only the drive of money. Human relations never entered his thinking — he had built PSI through ruthlessness, hard work and courageous, calculated risk-taking.

'We should have backed the Ecological Lobby, given them millions, fostered their violence…' Browne was spitting the words; '…too late now. I tell you, Knud…'

But Kartar lapsed again into silence, his eyes following the smoke spiralling to the ceiling. That small, full-lipped mouth, pursed like a child's, was deceptive. His black eyes, restless in the sallow face, never met Knud's gaze. And Browne tolerated Knud Carlsen because the Dane was useful to him; human feelings did not come into it. Knud could do all the dirty work and he smiled to himself — it was worth the occasional humiliation for the money Kartar paid him.

'I tell you, Knud, between these four walls, I wish I'd never built the ULCCs. The one mistake I've ever made.'

Knud had never seen this other side of the bustling, confident chairman. He had made his money quickly by buying up condemned tankers from the scrapyards, ships which even the Greeks would not use. 'A ship has to have a last owner,' was the adage in the marine world — and Kartar Browne was usually behind the clapped-out ships. His name stank in the shipping world and not only because of the state of his ships which he insured only nominally. He refused to operate them under IMCO (Inter-Governmental Maritime Consultative Organization) auspices; his ships sailed only under flags of convenience — Panama, Liberia, Moravia and all the rest. By so doing, he need man them only with uncertificated crews, men who would work the ships for their keep and pocket-money — Cypriots, Filipinos, Malaysians, the poor devils. These underpaid crews were outside the ITWF'S (International Transport Workers' Federation) jurisdiction. They were not unionized but, at least, they were better off than in their own countries, or they would never put to sea in Planeka's fleet. Carlsen had learnt to ask no questions, nor to offer his opinion...

'Things should get better, sir,' he said. 'For years to come the industrial nations won't be able to run their economies on nuclear power alone. They'll still need crude oil.'

'I should never have listened to the experts. I did not take enough trouble, give enough thought to *Leviathan* and *Goliath*'s design. Their tank disposition is wrong. Operators need to vary their cargoes when they charter a ship now.'

Carlsen would always remember *Leviathan*'s launching day. As the huge dock had filled, the great ship, the first of a new generation of Ultra Large Crude Carriers (ULCCs), had floated exactly to her marks, a triumph for three years of design work. When loaded with her 586,000 tonnes of crude, she would displace 674,026 tonnes, the largest ship in the world. With her laden draught of 104 feet (17 fathoms, 2 feet), her economical speed was 17.8 knots, better than her designed speed. In ballast she could knock up 19.2 knots, a justification for Kartar Browne's faith in nuclear marine engineering.

It was an open secret that the Americans had built the ship to provide work for their yards; the finance terms had been slanted to induce Browne to place his order in the States. He had countered the Americans' insistence that *Leviathan* should have innumerable and complicated safety measures before she would be allowed to discharge in American waters by providing minimal accommodation standards (no library, no cinema space); he had also cut the communication equipment and the fitting of expensive satellite navigational gear to a minimum. He had abandoned the proposal to fit the inclined rudders as fitted in *Batillus* and *Bellamya*, the first ULCCs which Shell had built; the cost was not worth the reduced stopping distances which these novel rudders gave, Browne had declared.

In spite of these economies, *Leviathan*, and now her sistership, *Goliath*, were miracles of modern nuclear and electronic engineering. Her four nuclear reactors cooked her four boilers. These each developed 34,000 HP which in turn powered the four turbines and four propellers. Knud would not forget launching day and the trials that followed — the ships were years ahead of their time, but already they were nearly obsolete — Kartar Browne was dreaming of using a development of ZETA to drive his next ships: boiler and turbine stages would be eliminated and the shafts be driven directly by electrical power through gigantic electric motors.

'Another port, Knud?' Kartar pushed the decanter across the table. 'I've got to cut running costs. Any ideas?'

'You can't reduce any more on the manning side, sir. *Goliath* is already working watch-and-watch; officers, particularly the juniors and fifth engineers, are almost unobtainable these days, even if you pay top rates.'

Knud knew that he had miscalculated — the smirk of satisfaction vanished from Browne's face. The attraction to work these modern monsters was eroded by the long hours and bad pay which Browne imposed. Trouble was simmering in one of the older ships, *Sumba*. The unions had blacklisted her in Middlesbrough when the master had refused to discuss matters with the local boys. Knud sighed; if it wasn't for his good salary … every man had his price, they said.

'I pay too much for docking and bottom-cleaning,' Browne snapped. 'The speed of the marine growth is terrifying, working these tropical waters. The Americans know that I can dock only in their graving dock. I don't enjoy being held to ransom.' He turned and faced Knud. 'This is where I can save money. Any ideas?'

Knud Carlsen saw in his imagination the vast area of red plating, when he had walked beneath the giants, as they were building in the dock. And then he remembered an advertisement he had seen in the trade paper, when he had felt bloody-minded last month. He had been tempted to quit and start up on his own — an underwater bottom-cleaning and anti-fouling company was up for sale somewhere in the west country.

'Ships' bottoms can be anti-fouled underwater these days. You know that, sir?'

Browne nodded irritably. 'But is the technique efficient? How long does the anti-fouling last? What are the costs?' He was firing the questions at Knud, a sure sign that he was searching for confirmation about something. 'Find out the answers, Carlsen. If they make sense, we'll go into the anti-fouling business ourselves … I could save millions…'

Knud curbed his irritation. More urgent problems were brewing: 'What do you want me to do about *Sumba*, sir?

Captain van Hoëk phoned me from Rotterdam, after he had slipped his ship himself from Middlesbrough on the midnight tide. His Chinese crew are giving trouble.'

Kartar Browne had pushed back his chair, all of his five feet three bristling with anger. 'That's what I pay you for, Carlsen. Deal with it, any way you like.' The sallow face had shut, close as an oyster. 'Don't let the lazy bastards hold up Planeka's programme.'

'Right, sir.' Carlsen pushed back his chair, thankful for the chance to get away. 'I must say goodnight to your wife. Thanks for a good evening.'

The Rover purred, the gravel spurted as he let in the clutch; he watched Mrs Browne, a picture of relaxed elegance in her pale apricot sari, raising her hand as he disappeared down the drive; there was no sign of her husband.

He had not told Kartar that he had already made up his mind over *Sumba*. He would show the whole fleet who was boss, whatever the consequences. He had already begun searching for someone with resolution to take charge of 'Operation Take-Over', as he had called it when he had drafted his orders. He had to find the right man quickly, or the whole plan might misfire; the leader for whom he was looking had to be physically and mentally tough, someone with service training who would obey orders and who would not allow scruples to interfere with the objective. He had already told his secretary to advertise the job nationally and he was interviewing the shortlist in the morning.

He swung the Rover onto the B1197. He would pick up the motorway and belt down it for the tunnel. Maya refused to leave their pleasant house on the outskirts of Chislehurst, even for that megalomaniac, Kartar Browne. She was one of the few women whom Knud knew who declared frankly that she lived only for material things. She accepted the good things of life without asking how he earned the money to pay for them. He had never told her he was mortgaged to the hilt and he never would, whilst she remained with him. His past was too murky for comfort and he was loath to lose her. He smiled as he lit up another cigar from the lighter on the dashboard. The tip glowed in the semi-darkness; the car responded and he felt the pressure of acceleration in the small of his back. He smiled in anticipation: he would be home within the hour and Maya would be waiting for him.

CHAPTER 5

'Fasten your seat belts, please. No smoking.'

The clipped accent of the KLM hostess was pleasantly relaxed. David Krivine wedged himself comfortably against the back of his seat as the jets whined and the 727 began taxiing towards the runway.

'The swiftest pier-head jump I've ever had,' he remarked to his second-in-command, Paul Bland, who was sitting beside him. 'Never thought I'd make Heathrow on time.'

'Carlsen calls us his "commando",' Bland said. 'Uses us for all sorts of jobs. We've been on standby for this *Sumba* caper for ten days now.' He nodded towards the twenty-three men sitting in the block of seats reserved for them by Planeka; 'They're all ex-SAS and Royal Marines. Carlsen pays well, but they drink most of it away.' Bland smiled bleakly as the aircraft began plunging down the runway. The tail lifted, the fuselage took on its angle and they were clambering into the sky.

In the enforced silence, David Krivine relived the last hectic forty-eight hours: the summons to London following his phone call in answer to the intriguing press advert. He had barely time to throw his steaming-bag together before Sally was driving him to Aberdeen airport to catch the last flight of the day.

'Hope to have good news for you when you get back,' she had said. 'With your father's backing, the bank won't let you down. I'm going down, anyway, to have a look at the Trefusis cottage,' she said as she kissed him.

'I'll keep in touch with Jonathan. Phone him when you get back or if you need anything. Take care...' He could still see in his mind her tiny figure standing by the fence as the plane trundled down the Aberdeen runway.

The interview with Carlsen, operations manager of Planeka Shipping International at their offices in Clapham, had been surprisingly brief. By his accent and with his heavy, Scandinavian face, a Swede or a Dane, perhaps, he had chain-smoked throughout the twenty minutes. The brittle, blue eyes had left David with an uncomfortable feeling — a callous man, out of condition, but efficient — a man who knew what he wanted. The small, full-lipped mouth was unpleasantly moist and red. He was as tall as David, but probably in his early forties. Whether David liked Carlsen or not was immaterial: Carlsen had offered him the job. 'I'll pay you a thousand quid, cash, if you get *Sumba* to sea without trouble. Half now, half on completion. With your background, Mr Krivine, you should know how to obey orders without asking questions.' His mouth had pursed sarcastically as he had hoisted his bulk from the desk. He had extracted five hundred pounds in ten pound notes from a wall safe in the office which, surprisingly for such a large company, was so unpretentious. 'The twenty-three-man relief crew, under their bosun, Paul Bland, will be at Heathrow for the 15.15 Rotterdam flight. Act as you think best, Krivine. Succeed, that's all I need from you. Sign here for the cash...' — and the interview had ended.

'When will you speak to the crew?' Bland asked as the 727 levelled off at 28,000 feet. 'I've told 'em you're the boss. They'll do what they're told, provided they're sober.'

For the rest of the flight, David laid his plans, checking and double-checking with Bland the facts as they knew them. David had spoken to the master of the ship and Captain van Hoëk was expecting the relief crew this evening. His Chinese crew were refusing to work *Sumba* who, having discharged her crude at the terminal, had been blacklisted by the Rotterdam dockies. They would sail her when they were paid a better rate — that negotiated by the International Transport Workers' Federation. They were also demanding over two month's back pay due to them. Fortunately, communications still remained open through the bosun who could speak a little English.

'Only as a last resort are you to use force, Bland,' David said quietly. 'Things are bloody enough as they are, without risking the blacklisting of Planeka. Tell your blokes to take it easy.'

Paul Bland's reply was unintelligible, as the hostess garbled through the communication system. Through the window, David saw the Rotterdam tower reaching towards the circling plane.

'I'll speak to the lads in the bus,' David said. 'Tell them to be as unobtrusive as they can. We'll wait outside the docks until dusk.' The only Chinaman on deck slid from the shadows after the last of David Krivine's party had crossed the gangway. The seaman was disappearing through the door from which the varnish had long since peeled, when Bland barred his way.

'We're the relief crew,' he said. 'Take us to the bosun.' The slight, middle-aged Chinaman in the blue dungarees nodded, his eyes impassive. He glided through the door, Bland and six men following him, after they had dumped their gear on the deck. The remainder of Carlsen's commando went silently to their allotted stations. David felt sorry for anyone who might get in their way; they were a brutish lot, in comparison to the mild man conducting Bland down to the crew's saloon.

Sumba was an old ship, probably one of the leftovers from Hitler's war. Her bridge structure was forward, the lights from the officers' cabins beginning to glow in the darkening dusk. David could leave the take-over to Bland, while he sought the master — but he had been a naïve fool to have allowed his thugs to while away the time in the bar outside the docks. As he began following the pipelines forward, along the upper deck, he spotted a figure watching him from the starboard wings of the bridge. David hurried onwards and, as he began mounting the ladders, the tall officer came down to meet him:

'Captain van Hoëk,' a guttural voice said. 'I'm glad you've come, Mr Krivine. This way to my cabin.'

During the next half-hour, the master presented his officers, the only other Dutchman being the mate. They spoke English and David soon learned the facts: the Chinese bosun, a reasonable man, had been unable to contain the crew's grievances any longer. At the Isle of Grain, one of the crew had contacted the Chinese grapevine and their complaints had been passed on to an official of the Transport and General Workers' Union. London headquarters had ordered the blacklisting of the ship if the master, on orders from his owners, still refused to discuss the complaints about the abysmally low rates of pay. Captain van Hoëk, a stubborn, hard-drinking type by the look of him, had slipped *Sumba* on the night tide and had vanished into the grey waters of the North Sea. Through a link call Carlsen had ordered him to proceed to Rotterdam to discharge his crude.

The Rotterdam terminal had accepted the ship and the master had managed, for once, to keep the pumps going long enough to discharge the cargo before the news reached the ITWF'S Dutch office. The ship was in ballast but unable to sail: her Chinese crew had had enough. They were gambling happily in their saloon and would continue to do so until their pay was improved.

David did not like Bols and needed a clear head. He put down his empty glass and extracted a file from his steaming-bag. 'Here you are, Captain. The crew's discharge: their contracts with Planeka are terminated.'

The Hollander showed little emotion: 'So your men are my new crew, yes? You are the company's agent, Krivine? Or are you my new bosun?' He swallowed the Dutch gin in one.

'No, sir,' David said. 'I don't like this any more than you do. Officially, Paul Bland is your new bosun. Mr Carlsen told me to ask you to sail immediately. He wants you outside territorial waters as rapidly as possible. He'll then give you fresh sailing orders — Venezuela probably.'

'And my Chinese crew?'

'My orders are to get them ashore tonight... run them off, if need be.'

At that moment they heard excitable voices approaching from the upper deck. The mate heaved himself from his chair and opened the door. Bland, holding a Chinaman by the neck, was remonstrating with the bosun who was insisting on seeing the master.

'What's the trouble, Mr Bland?' David snapped. The wriggling seaman spat out a tooth which bloodied the white paintwork on the cabin bulkhead. A flap of skin hung from his lip and an angry weal showed across the pronounced cheekbone.

'He tried to knife one of my men,' Bland rasped. 'This bastard's earned what's come to him.'

The elderly bosun removed his Mao cap as he stood before his captain.

'You pay month's wages, Captain. We go ashore, right now. Company fly crew back Shanghai? Bosun Tsing Fu want no trouble... You fly us, Captain?'

Van Hoëk strolled to the safe on the bulkhead and extracted a bundle of greenbacks.

'I've got it ready for you, Bosun,' he said, without rancour. 'Muster the crew aft and the mate will pay you now. I can't promise about the flights.'

'You ring head office?'

'Yes, Bosun.' Van Hoëk held out his hand. 'Good luck, Tsing Fu. When will you and the crew be ready to leave the ship? I must catch this tide.'

'Tsing Fu go now, Captain. Friends ready go too…' The dignified and loyal Chinaman stepped backwards from the cabin.

An embarrassed silence followed, as Bland pushed his prisoner through the door. 'Good riddance, Captain,' he said. 'I'll report as soon as all the crew have gone. We'll work the ship as soon as you're ready.' He turned to the chief officer: 'Your new bosun, sir,' he guffawed, as he cut him off an exaggerated salute.

David turned to van Hoëk. 'When will you sail, sir?'

'As soon as Customs have cleared us. Thanks for your help, Mr Krivine.' The master made towards the cabin door. 'You're flying back?'

'Next flight, Captain,' David said. 'I'm glad it's worked out.' He felt uncomfortable, troubled by what he had organized. 'I hope the company will fly them back to China.'

Van Hoëk fixed him with an angry stare. 'If Planeka refuses,' he said, 'Browne's fleet, or that part of it that's Chinese manned, will be crippled throughout the world. You know what they're like: the Chinese grapevine beats our unions hollow.'

David picked up his bag, the master following him to the gangway.

'Tell 'em that in London,' were van Hoëk's parting words. 'Fly my crew home or there'll be trouble.'

CHAPTER 6

'Yes, Mr Krivine,' the secretary was saying, 'I'll tell Mr Jonathan you've called,' and the female at the other end of the telephone laughed pleasantly, '...you're sure you've got Mrs Grant's message right, sir?'

'I'm to phone the Falmouth bank manager at once; and Mrs Grant is at Trefusis. Thanks a lot.'

David fumbled in his pockets but he had insufficient ten-pence pieces to get through to Falmouth. An impatient queue was building up outside his kiosk in the Heathrow arrivals lounge, so he reluctantly surrendered the phone and hurried to the tobacco shop opposite.

'We don't give change,' the spotty assistant snapped, as she continued giggling with her boyfriend who was sprawled across the counter.

'Where, then ... please?' David asked. This could only be Heathrow. The girl nodded towards the queues milling around the exchange counters.

'Try them.'

Civility cost nothing, but he was irritable after these past forty-eight hours. He had missed the last flight and had been forced to spend the night at a grubby boarding house in Rotterdam. He had roused out at five this morning to catch the early flight, but it was already 09.15 here, Heathrow time. Ten minutes later he was shoving ten-pence pieces into the phone box ... the Falmouth line clicked.

'Yes, Mr Krivine, this is the manager speaking. When can you come and see me?'

'Late this afternoon, if that's convenient to you. I'm catching the first train down…' He paused and added, 'You can manage the loan?'

'It's not as easy as that, Mr Krivine, I'm afraid. We'll talk when we meet this evening, shall we?'

He hung up, his future still hazy. He would take a taxi, whatever it cost, and nip out to Clapham for the balance of the money Carlsen owed him: five hundred quid would come in handy at the moment, if the manager was prepared to play — and if Hull Cleaning Services was still for sale.

David sensed things were not right when he entered Carlsen's office. He kept David on his feet and the Dane looked embarrassed, sourer than at their last meeting. So *Sumba* had not sailed?

'I took over the ship,' David said. 'The Chinese went ashore quietly in the end. When I left, van Hoëk was about to sail with Bland as bosun.'

'*Sumba* got away okay,' Carlsen said.

'The Chinese insisted on being flown home. They stood by their contract. I told the master I'd emphasize their request to you.'

'The owner refuses to fly them back to China. They've broken their contract with us by refusing to work.'

David felt the anger smouldering within him.

'We gave our word,' he said. 'We told them they'd be flown home, if they left the ship quietly.'

'You had no authority to do so. Mr Browne — he's my boss and the owner — isn't pleased at all, Krivine.' Carlsen glared at him, then began pacing the floor of his diminutive office. 'He has already telexed the agent to refuse the Chinese demands.'

'It's their right…'

Carlsen broke in angrily: 'It's none of your business. You've made a balls-up of the whole operation. You've cost the company a tidy packet.'

'How the hell?' David shouted. 'We got the ship to sea.'

'And stopped five others. The Chinese have blacklisted all the Planeka ships. They're refusing to work until *Sumba*'s crew are flown home. Bloody awful mess.' He stared hard at Krivine, his ponderous jaw set like a mole trap.

'I've finished my part of the bargain, Carlsen,' David retorted, the blood pumping in his temples. 'Pay me the five hundred pounds you owe me.'

The corners of Carlsen's small mouth were twitching. 'Mr Browne has vetoed the final payment,' he sneered. 'I would pay you, but he's forbidden me to. He tells me you've failed to carry out your part satisfactorily.'

David clouted the corner of the desk. 'Take me to Mr Bloody Browne.'

'He won't see you. Sees no one, except through me. I'm really sorry, Krivine, but there's nothing I can do.' The Dane began to push back his chair. 'I've a lot to do this morning,' and he flipped through a pile of correspondence, as he touched the bell-push on his desktop. 'Show Mr Krivine out, Miss Hewitt, please.'

David had sufficient control not to strike the man behind the desk. Carlsen was spreading out his hands, shrugging his shoulders. 'Sorry, Mr Krivine. I would if I could...' and his words echoed all the way to Paddington. The last coach of the Penzance express was disappearing at the end of the platform when David finally dashed on to the platform.

The next train left in an hour's time. He would have a beer to calm himself down; he might just make the Falmouth bank before the manager left at the end of the day.

She had given up hope that David could be home for the night and had locked up, when she heard him thumping on the cottage door.

'Coming…'

Then she was in his arms and suddenly the world's cares vanished… She drew away from him to read his face; he was incapable of hiding anything from her.

'What's the manager say? How did the trip go?' She buried her head in his chest again. 'I'm so happy you're home,' she said. 'I was worried.'

He freed himself gently, a half-smile on his tired face: 'It's like the two old Jew boys in hospital,' he said. 'Good news and bad news. I'll give you the bad news first.'

'No,' she laughed, happy again. 'Let's have the story.'

He dropped his bag and slumped on to the kitchen chair. He pulled her on to his knee, stroked her hair, as he re-told the old chestnut — he had a wealth of stories, good and less good…

'Ikey was an old man,' he began, 'and he was in hospital. The surgeon had just done his rounds when Ikey's oldest friend arrived at his bedside during visiting hours.

'"How are you, Ikey?" he asked. "You look unhappy."

'"Not too good," said Ikey. "I've good news and bad for you. Which would you like first, old friend?"

'"The bad news, Ikey. Give me the bad news first."

'"They're going to take off my left foot, Eli."

'"That's bad," Eli said, shaking his head. "Now for the good news…?"

'"I'm giving you my left slipper."'

'That's sick,' Sally chuckled. 'Let's have the bad news…'

'That *Sumba* job turned sour. They're only paying me the first five hundred pounds — the bastards.'

'Better than nothing,' she said quietly. 'What about the good news?'

He rose from the chair, picked her up like a child and set her down before him so that he could watch her:

'The bank is giving us the loan… We've got the loan, my Sal, but there's a snag.' He enfolded her in his arms again. 'They've reduced the loan to £9,000. I must repay it within three years by making regular repayments.'

'You can't expect much else, David. You can buy Hull Cleaning then?' She gave a cry of delight as he pulled her to the doorway. 'Let's go down and see our new firm before the sun sets,' he said.

'Yes, let's — and you still haven't shown me the new terminal. I've been so busy getting the cottage ready for you, I've been to the town only once. I can get most things in Flushing.'

She drove the old van herself, told him of her decision to sell the Aberdeen business now that he was launching Hull Cleaning Services. She took the back road through Tregew to reach the creek. It was high water and his sixty feet of waterfront looked attractive, in spite of the tumbledown shed and decrepit yard. They clambered through the broken-down fence; muck and debris were everywhere, but he was immediately enthusing over his plans, how he would build his 'crawlers'. He was an overgrown schoolboy, home for the holidays. She gripped his hand, trying to preserve this moment for ever. 'I'll have my office here,' she said. 'I'll keep your accounts straight. You needn't worry, you'll be able to concentrate and get on with what you love doing…'

'Diving,' he said, and he crushed her fingers in his huge hand. 'Sal, I'll be diving again…'

It was past ten when they threaded through Penryn and drove south, around the back of Falmouth to Pendennis Point. Dusk was falling and the castle reared above them, gaunt against the crimson sky. The magnificent harbour of Falmouth and Carrick Roads stretched to the northward, shimmering indigo-blue on this windless night. Sally nestled into his shoulder as they stood overlooking Falmouth Bay which was to become their life. Below them a trail of gulls was flapping towards the lighthouse of St Anthony Head, its white sector already occulting every twenty seconds.

'There it is,' he murmured. 'Pencra — the new terminal.'

To the southward, a long, concrete breakwater stretched into the bay, parallel with the coast. A gap showed at its southern end, where another mole ran east and west towards Manacle Point, that dark headland which concealed Coverack and Black Head from their sight.

'D'you see the bridge connecting the southern mole to Manacle Point?' David said. 'They built that first, just north of the rocks. There's a two-way road on it now, leading out to the fuelling derricks on the southern arm for the smaller tankers. The big boys use the northern mole and the two terminal buoys. Look, Sal, you can just see their quick-flashing lights — inside the north-south breakwater.'

He was a new man, here on the coast, close again to the sea which was his life. He would become part of this new terminal when HCS began operating.

'They've taken nearly seven years to build Pencra,' he said. 'It'll change the whole face of the west, now that the Celtic and new fields are coming on stream. The ULCCs can discharge at these buoys, outside the thirty-fathom line.'

She took his arm, gently turned him towards the van.

'Tell me the rest tomorrow,' she said. 'When we can see it all in daylight. I've got to go back to Aberdeen, David. It'll take a little time to wind up the business.'

'By the time you get back,' he said, 'I'll have Hull Cleaning Services operating. You'll see, Sal.'

She left him alone with his thoughts, while she drove him back to Fuchsia Cottage. Perhaps the chip on his shoulder would vanish, this bitterness diminish. Perhaps he could dismiss his hates: bureaucracy, dictatorial unions outside the law, the computerizing of humanity...

He realized, she knew, what she was renouncing to share her life with him. She was fully committed now, bound to him, this man she loved, however unreliable, unstable he was. She would try to make him happy, give him all she knew, cherish this man. Dear God, how she loved him. She touched his sleeve, wondering whether they would ever again attain such peace, be so in love...

CHAPTER 7

Jeremy Pedrick hurried towards Lime Street. He detested unpunctuality, particularly as he had this vital meeting at 11.30 this morning with Lethbridge and Seymour. Jonathan Krivine would be at his box: he was never late.

Pedrick paused to check his appearance in the tobacconist's window: rotund, balding fair hair and puffy beneath the eyes, his twelve years with his Lloyd's brokers, Sturgess, Hardy and Boldre, were beginning to leave their mark. He enjoyed his work as a broker: he relished the cut-and-thrust of the market place, handling these vast sums of money; he felt a quiet pride in the integrity that was the vital element in being a good broker. Being a slick operator got you nowhere with Lloyd's, as several of his contemporaries had discovered to their cost. Jeremy adjusted his sombre tie and hastened towards the impressive portal that was the entrance to the world's largest marine insurance market.

A gleaming blue Rolls was waiting outside; its engine purred as it drove off, the chairman and vice-chairman, grey haired and distinguished, talking to each other in the rear seats. This display of wealth lent a dignity which was entirely becoming to this ancient institution. The public, erroneously sometimes, held a prejudiced opinion of Lloyd's, but nowadays the wearing of an old school tie was almost a disadvantage. He had come from a comprehensive school background, as had so many of the new generation of brokers' underwriters. They were as successful as their forebears, and, curiously, were as proud of their Lloyd's tradition, as passionate in defending its privileges and reputation against an uninformed, and sometimes envious, proletariat.

'Good morning, Mr Pedrick.'

The waiter at the entrance was an imposing figure in his white shirt, black tie, and scarlet cloak with black velvet collar. Lloyd's could not operate with such smoothness, but for the efficiency of its 'waiters'. Merchants and sea captains had met three centuries ago at Lloyd's Coffee House to conduct their business in congenial surroundings — the ale houses and taverns were not so conducive to clear-thinking when placing insurance risks.

Present-day Lloyd's had journeyed far since then — its business representing nearly five million pounds in premiums each working day. Without the superintendent and his waiters the Room would be unworkable. Jeremy was convinced that it was right for this great corporation to guard its heritage jealously. The magnificence of the Committee Room represented Lloyd's secure position in the business world — it was one of the most beautiful rooms which Jeremy had the privilege ever to have seen. Its elegant ceiling had come from Bowood House in Wiltshire, a masterpiece of tracery in pastel shades which was matched by the decoration of the hall outside. Three exquisite crystal chandeliers scintillated from that incomparable ceiling — it was truly a room fit to receive Her Majesty, the Queen Mother, when she visited the corporation as an honorary member.

Jeremy Pedrick had six minutes in hand, so he decided to have a glance at the Casualty Board. He had already had a tough morning, gathering Planeka Shipping International's final proposals together: Kartar Browne had become a notoriously hard bargainer in the shipping world. The bad boy was insisting on some unusual conditions, but (without the knowledge of the underwriters) he was prepared to accept a higher rate to obtain his requirements. He, Jeremy, would suggest a three per cent rate ... these new nuclear ULCCs were an unknown and, potentially, a much higher risk than the VLCCs who had now been cured of their original troubles. It had taken the disaster of *Matra* off the Cape to prove that the VLCCs had originally been rated too cheaply. Underwriters were not likely to repeat their error for the ULCCs.

Pedrick was overloaded with work: the telexes on his desk this morning had taken over two hours to sift. Quotations for various risks originated from all sources: owners wanted a rate for the risk involved, and these were very varied. When he had dealt with his own telex, he just had time to complete his 'slip' for Planeka. He was thankful that he had already consulted Krivine: but Browne's latest condition, that *Leviathan* should be covered by the time she slipped from the Sea Island terminal buoy on her next trip from Kharg Island, was pushing the syndicates — they needed more time when quoting a rate for such an unknown and colossal risk as these nuclear ULCCs. He hoped that Krivine, who was now dealing solely with the Planeka enquiry on behalf of Lethbridge and Seymour's syndicate, would agree a three per cent rate — and sign his initials on the 'slip'.

Pedrick had had a bellyful of the *Leviathan* affair; but these protracted negotiations could be carried out best by brokers — which was why Lloyd's men would write their names on the line of the broker's slip ('underwrite'), only if the owner proceeded through a Lloyd's broker. The owner was then sure of a better deal than if he tried negotiating directly with underwriters — but a broker had to be vigilant these days, with the fierce competition they were facing from the Americans and Japanese. Underwriting principles had changed little in three hundred years: the broker sought the best price for his client — the underwriter negotiated for the highest rate he could win for his syndicate.

In the old building at Leadenhall Street, the atmosphere in the summer had been unbearably hot and humid: the caller suffered greatly in his throat from his continuous broadcasting — he required a special brand of tenacity to chant names for hours on end, in the traditional and doleful intonation wherein the last syllable of the name was accentuated and raised in tone. A broker or an underwriter would always catch his name, even above the murmur filling the Room — and even between eleven-fifteen and noon, and four o'clock and four-fifteen, when business was at its most brisk — an ability which applied also to the newest innovation, the lady members.

Jeremy Pedrick glanced again at the Casualty Board — he could identify none of his clients' vessels in the various messages pinned on the board or tick-ticking from the machines...

The Room was as busy as Jonathan Krivine had ever seen it. The marine market was buzzing with rumour. Something big was in the air and the ripples were spreading throughout the market. He paused for a moment at his box — life was becoming so hectic that, if he was not careful, he would lose that precious quality needed by good underwriters: the ability to think.

Lloyd's of London was an incredible place; certainly the most competitive market in the world, its individuality and flexibility being its strength. No one had yet bettered the definition of insurance as drafted by the unknown parliamentary lawyers who had drawn up the act during the reign of Queen Elizabeth I ... 'it cometh to pass that on loss or perishing of any ship there followeth not the undoing of any man, but the loss lighteth rather easily upon many than heavilie upon fewe…'

The principle remained today as it had been three centuries ago, whereby a Lloyd's policy was subscribed by private individuals with unlimited liability — but business and the market had grown to gigantic proportions since Edward Lloyd first provided his congenial coffee house.

A member had to be elected by the committee and had to show wealth of at least £75,000. His entire fortune was liable to meet any claims against him. Today there were nearly 10,000 members of Lloyd's and there were over three hundred syndicates, some with hundreds of names, others with only a few. A Lloyd's policy now was the same as it had always been — a hallmark of integrity.

Jonathan Krivine looked up from his desk. The Room was packed today — if business continued to expand, Lloyd's would have to seek further space — a historical problem which had plagued underwriters for three centuries. The caller was in his rostrum, a majestic figure, where he sat beneath the Lutine bell.

Jonathan felt a quiet pride in being a name in Lethbridge and Seymour's syndicate. He was particularly glad that he specialized in the marine side of insurance, although the aviation and motor business had swelled to immense proportions. He was a traditionalist at heart; he believed deeply that Lloyd's strength was its individuality and the loyalty of its members to the corporate body which had evolved during the centuries through competition and enterprise.

As he gazed across the Room, glad for an instant to ease his saturated brain, he caught sight of the wine-coloured waistcoat of Jeremy Pedrick threading its way through the press to the Casualty Board. He hoped the broker had his slip ready this morning because, he, Jonathan, had a mountain of work to complete before meeting David at the club tonight. He had tried to dissuade him, but David had insisted on coming up from Falmouth this evening: 'It's desperately important to me,' he had phoned. 'I need your help, Johnny.'

Why, in heaven's name, did David always choose these impossible moments? He assumed the world revolved around his personal difficulties, quagmires which he had usually constructed himself ... but, weakly, Jonathan had agreed to meet him for dinner after finishing in the Room. He had rung Sheppey and told Margaret that he could not be home tonight. She would run across to her mother in Gillingham, taking Katie, who was sickening for the measles, with her.

Things had begun to move at the New Year when Jeremy Pedrick had hinted that something was in the wind. Today was Monday, 14 March, and a fortnight ago Jeremy had first presented his broker's slip: an order for cover of the largest risk ever offered in maritime insurance. The ship was the largest man-made moving object; then add to that risk her nuclear-powered propulsion... Lethbridge and Seymour were to be the leading syndicate; Lethbridge had taken Jonathan off all other work, in order to concentrate upon the broker's enquiry.

Though everything had pointed towards Planeka Shipping International, it was not until Jeremy had formally presented his slip at Jonathan's box that the identity of the potential assurer was known: Kartar Browne, that mysterious figure in the shipping world. Though Planeka had originally been compelled by the Americans to insure Browne's two nuclear-powered monsters, *Leviathan* and *Goliath*, in the States, the contract date was running out.

Browne was seeking the re-insurance at Lloyd's for two stated reasons: he was profoundly pro-British; and, with the recent outbreak of oil-tanker hijacking, he feared the vulnerability of his two gargantuan nuclear crude carriers. Only at Lloyd's, he felt, could he find the cover he needed for war risks, civil strife and piracy on the high seas — at a reasonable premium. Only at Lloyd's could the colossal value of these two ships be dispersed safely across the market. Only at Lloyd's, with its prestige and vast resources (almost every large passenger aircraft which flew was insured at Lloyd's) could Kartar Browne hope to find the cover he wanted.

The enquiry was firm, Jeremy Pedrick had said. Would Lethbridge's syndicate write a line? Kartar Browne was in a hurry and needed the cover by the time his first ship, *Leviathan*, next loaded at Kharg Island, off Iran, sometime at the end of April or beginning of May. She was now battling with storms, force 12, north of the Azores, on her first trip to Falmouth Bay. The press would be there to watch the world's largest ship pick up for the first time her terminal buoy at Pencra. Kartar Browne would be there, too, incognito: he wanted to see for himself how his captain and his colossal ship would perform.

Browne had already leaked to his brokers that, if the operational results proved satisfactory, he intended placing a further order for two more nuclear ULCCs, *Colossus* and *Mastodon*, to be powered by the recent EEC propulsion breakthrough: nuclear-reactors and ZETA direct electrical drive.

It was not surprising that Lethbridge was pulling out all the stops; but the rate which the syndicate had to propose must be realistic: underwriters had taken serious losses when the VLCCs had first appeared in the late sixties — if the rate was too low, a loss would shake the marine market to its foundations…

Jeremy was picking his way through the throng. He, Jonathan, would nip across to have a word with Robert, the Casualty Book clerk, after Jeremy had finished…

'Haven't got much time, Jeremy,' he said, as the broker came and sat beside him at the box. 'Any fresh facts for me?'

'Our client isn't the easiest of men,' Pedrick said. 'But he agrees to a one-year cover, the premium and risks to be reviewed again within twelve months.'

'Our syndicate insists on this, I'm afraid. There are too many imponderables. If he's happy on a one-year policy, then we can go ahead and complete the cover.'

'Browne wants total cover from the moment *Leviathan* slips from her buoy, or he'll go elsewhere. He's arranged for his present American cover to remain until the ship slips from the Sea Island terminal at Kharg Island.'

'Lethbridge has agreed, providing a Lloyd's surveyor can sail with her to do the round trip in her from Pencra to Kuwait and back. That's the only way we can really judge a risk of this magnitude, Jeremy. Will Browne agree?'

'It's a reasonable request. The surveyor will have to join her at Pencra tomorrow or the next day, if he is to do the round trip.'

Jonathan smiled, stuck out his chest: 'We feel it would be a good thing if the surveyor could meet the owners direct. I'd like to go down to Falmouth tomorrow.'

'*You're* the surveyor or whatever you like to be called … *you?*' Jeremy's mouth was hanging open.

Jonathan was laughing. 'Hardly complimentary, Jeremy. I'm their Lloyd's man, that's all. They haven't given me a title. Underwriters naturally want the facts on a revolutionary ship of this nature. With her sister-ship, *Goliath*, they're the biggest risk Lloyd's has ever considered. Only fair, isn't it?'

'We've given you all we know, but it isn't much. Trials, facts and figures, statistics…'

'We must be certain about the crew and ship's officers. No one has sailed a ship as big as this before. She dwarfs even *Batillus*; she's a superb ship. And don't forget, Browne insists on sailing them under the Panamanian flag.' Jonathan rose from his seat, squeezed past his colleagues to escape the disconcerting chatter around him.

'Over there, Jeremy, where we can think. By the Casualty Book.' He had to get away from it all for a moment: his head was swimming.

'And supposing Browne refuses to have you on board?'

'No deal,' Jonathan snapped. 'Simple as that.'

CHAPTER 8

Jonathan Krivine stood behind the Casualty Book clerk and watched him writing up the most recent entry.

The clerk, who worked from the Intelligence Department, was in daily communication with the casualty reporting branch at Colchester. From their 'Bible', in which every marine incident in the world was recorded, he compiled his weekly casualty reports from the information which came in daily. Every marine disaster or potential disaster, every incident which might involve a claim from anywhere in the world, was entered by Robert Faulkner in his neat and stylish handwriting into the Casualty Book. Known as the Casualty Book clerk, he was a popular figure in the Room. Robert traced ships and entered up the major casualties. After his twelve years with Lloyd's, he had a rare skill; his disciplined service in the RAF perhaps had much to do with his uncanny flair.

'Morning, Mr Krivine,' he said, glancing up from his work. 'Won't be a minute...'

Robert Faulkner could smell out the shadier skulduggeries, sift the minor incidents from the potentially grave ... a hold full of jute burning in Saigon; a coaster with engine failure off Valparaiso; a cargo ship dragging her anchors and colliding with a South Korean coaster in Seoul. If a ship was drifting on to a lee shore and needed to be towed off with tug assistance, the local Lloyd's agent would soon be through on the line. The casualty reporting branch at Colchester knew the whereabouts of tugs throughout the world and would contact the Salvage Association for help. Robert had once been radio-telephoned direct from sea by a master who needed immediate towing assistance. Robert had rung through direct to the Salvage Association who had dispatched the nearest tug to pluck her from disaster.

'An interesting one here, Mr Krivine,' the Casualty Book clerk said, as he read out a message just handed to him. 'Not one of yours, I hope.'

The telex had come direct from the Salvage Officer in Taipeh: 'Unable to board pm, due to weather conditions,' Jonathan read. 'Will try again tomorrow. Consider paramount importance that engine-room should be pumped out as soon as possible. No suitable pumps are available locally.'

'Not one of ours, Robert.' Jonathan breathed with relief. 'What are her chances?'

'Not too good, but the Chinese Navy is assisting. The Hong Kong salvage officer is fully committed, so the Association is flying out one of their staff salvage officers. This one smells.'

'Why?'

'She's the steam tanker, *Kolag*, built in 1957. She's Chinese registered and sails under the so-called Somali flag of convenience. She's loaded and is on her last voyage before going in for break-up. Why has she gone aground, Mr Krivine?'

Jonathan felt sorry for the brokers and underwriters involved: this would be a difficult one to prove. With luck, they could escape the International Arbitration Courts at the Temple — a process which could drag on for years. Instead, the Salvage Association might be approached, which might give a ruling in this *Kolag* case. The two parties would try to compromise, if it was a genuine claim — but towing incidents were notoriously difficult to settle. If a tug caused damage in trying to pass a line or in getting alongside in bad weather — and eventually saved the ship — had the owners a case or not?

It was very difficult to prove whether a claim was a 'throwaway'; if it was, the owners would not get their money.

The *Berge Istra*, a supertanker of 223,913 tons, was the biggest loss so far for Lloyd's — one reason why underwriters usually insured only a proportion of the hull value, brokers placing elsewhere the remainder of the risk. The *Kriti Sun*, 123,000 tons, had taught that lesson: her hull was insured for thirty million dollars. The *Berge Istra* disappeared off the Philippines. Weeks later two survivors said that there had been an explosion. A possible cause was that, after tank cleaning, static electricity had built up in the tanks where gas, its pressure changed, provided a combustible mixture for the static electricity to cause the spark. Lloyd's paid up the claim for her hull value of 18.2 million dollars.

The cargo ship off the River Plate, carrying 3–4,000 head of sheep; the jute burning in a ship's hold in Saigon; the leaking seacock, later determined by the surveyors from Lloyd's Register in Fenchurch Street to be the cause of the total loss. Lloyd's paid up.

'*Great Bear*'s mine,' Jonathan said. 'Anything on her, Robert?'

'This was the last report we had…'

The handwritten entry was crisp, objective:

Date posted missing at Lloyd's: 5 Mar.
Name: Great Bear
Port of Registry: Panama
Tons Gross: 18,402
Tons Net: 11,213
No. of Crew: 35
Owners: Equator Steam Co.
Voyage: Sailed from Hull 7 Feb. for Charleston and last reported experiencing heavy weather about 25 miles SE Cape Cod at 1630 10

Her hull was in the usual millions of dollars — but the terrible ordeal of her drowning crews — where were the statistics for them? It was all so impersonal — Jonathan, an ex-seafarer, could see those furious seas, hear the gale roaring, the wind shrieking in the rigging … it was a pity more underwriters and brokers could not know what the sea was about. He turned to the Casualty Book clerk:

'Any decision yet, Robert?'

So much depended on the decision: she could be declared a CTL (Constructive Total Loss, when the cost of repairs would be greater than the actual hull value); a Total Loss; a Partial Loss; or a Compromised Loss.

'Nothing yet, Mr Krivine. But it's unusual to be so long without hearing anything.'

'It's a worry for us. Thanks, Robert.'

'Any time, Jonathan…'

The underwriter and the broker strolled back to the Lethbridge box. Pedrick was becoming impatient.

'Sorry, Jeremy. I was worried about *Great Bear*. Got your "slips"?'

'I think all's okay now.'

Jonathan perused the terms. The rate which Lethbridge's syndicate would set must reflect the risks which the broker's slip posed. Once they had agreed the rate between them, Jonathan could initial the line. The contract would then be honoured. What the ship comprised: cargo, tanker, container-ship… Her age? Size? Trade? Who were her owners and, most vitally, what was their record like? And, finally, were there any special conditions? Jonathan read the slip through again. The broker had added a time condition: *Leviathan* must be covered by the time she slipped from Kharg Island.

'This is pushing things a bit, Jeremy. If *Leviathan* hasn't been held up by the gale, she's due at Pencra on tomorrow's evening tide. That makes it the sixteenth of March. A few days to discharge and minor service — say, twentieth of March. That makes it about twentieth of April before she turns round again at Kharg Island … not much time.'

Pedrick was glancing at him, trying to read his mind; he was up to his tricks — no different to any good broker. But trust was the basis of the game…

'Browne will accept a Lloyd's representative on board,' Pedrick said, 'providing he can have the cover as he asks.'

'Right,' Jonathan said. 'What rate are you asking?'

'He's prepared to compromise after you and I last met. He appreciates that three per cent is too low for you, with the risks he is quoting. The rate is four per cent.'

'I want five.'

'No, Jonathan. My client can, and will, pay four. He's already met you halfway.'

Jonathan was prepared to compromise. He had received his instructions from Lethbridge, the underwriting agent for the syndicate, not to go lower than a minimum rate of four per cent. Lethbridge was the leading underwriter and with this 'lead' Jeremy could now approach the other syndicates to get his slip totally subscribed.

'Okay, Jeremy. I'll write my line.' He inscribed four per cent in clear figures, then scribbled his initials. 'Thanks for adding our conditions.'

'From the date of slipping from Kharg Island,' Jeremy repeated, 'and subject to your clause depending on the verdict of Lloyd's representative, at the end of the first half of the voyage. Okay, Johnny.' They shook hands. They knew they were setting the lead rate for the largest marine risk ever placed at Lloyd's. The remaining forty per cent of the risk was being placed elsewhere throughout the world — but that was the broker's business.

'Meet me for lunch?' Jeremy proposed.

'Can't manage it. I'm going down to Falmouth tomorrow.' He eased Jeremy out of the box. One thing at a time; he did not know how he could get through his work today… Jonathan Krivine slowly gathered his papers together, a frown creasing his forehead. He had not told Pedrick about his brother. He wished that he could have been frank with David; how much easier to have met together in Falmouth tomorrow, but Lloyd's were insisting on secrecy at this stage. He had begun to thread his way through the throng when the deep clang of the Lutine bell echoed through the Room.

The Room, which a second previously had been a buzzing market place, came to a standstill. All eyes were on the rostrum. The caller was reading from the message which he held before him. 'Ladies and gentlemen,' his deep voice intoned, 'two of the crew from the *Great Bear*, which sailed from Hull on the twenty-seventh of February, have been found in position forty miles south of Cape Cod. The sinking has been confirmed.'

The murmur in the Room gradually resumed. The day's business must continue. Jonathan's syndicate and many others would have to pay up. As he slowly wound his way towards the Captain's Room for a quick lunch, he could feel the bitter cold, see the ice building up on her upperworks… And tonight he would have to endure another frustrating meeting with his brother.

CHAPTER 9

Captain Giorgios Botsaris had to force himself out to the windward extremity of his bridge. Even behind this steel screen, he was forced to hold onto the lip of the starboard wing, for fear of being hurled against the after-screen. The barometer was certainly bearing out the storm warning which the radio officer had handed him during the afternoon.

Having no yardstick against which to measure the fury of this wind and sea, nothing except the crashing waves and the curtains of spume flying across the fo'c'sle-head, he felt an unusual unease deep inside him: he hated encountering a gale, with a long, moonless night ahead of him. He had ridden out a storm-force wind only once off Madagascar: he had hoped never to repeat again the experience of that cyclone... He remained in the port wing for a few seconds, long enough to glimpse the crimson slash of the sun setting behind the clouds sweeping up from the Azores. The sky was angry and there was an oppressive, humid stuffiness in the air. *Leviathan* was in for her first real blow...

Captain Botsaris scuttled back into the comfort of his luxurious bridge, the heart of this splendid vessel. He exulted in his ship: few men attained such heights of command. He smoothed back his ruffled black hair, a thick crop that was already, even at his relatively early age (he was only thirty-eight), silvering at the temples. He grasped the leading handrail as the ship shivered from stem to stern while she took a green sea amidships. He would leave the decision a little longer yet; he would have to heave-to until the worst was over.

So much depended on the mate and his Cargo Distribution Simulator (CDS). Even *Leviathan*, all 1,475 feet and 674,000 tons of her, moved about in the grip of an ocean gale. The suspicion of a smirk twitched the corners of his wide mouth as he watched the massive brass inclinometer canting slowly between five and ten degrees with each roll — this was the only instrument which could truly never fail. Gravity was reliable.

'Captain...'

He turned to see the overworked chief engineer standing by him. He was the only officer to wear uniform, a white boiler suit, his concession to tradition. The engineers' job was to keep the propulsion going, however many alarms bleeped in the Engine-Room Consol immediately behind the steering pulpit.

'Yes, Chief ... trouble?'

'Number two steering turbo-motor is overheating. I'll have to shut it down.' The chief was grey with weariness. He had been unable to sign on another fifth engineer last time in Venezuela, and his boys were stretched to the limit with their workload. The owner might have built the most complex and the biggest ships in the world; it was regrettable he had economized on the human element...

'All right, Stefan. I needed something to make up my mind. I'll come up to port and heave-to until this lot's over.' He turned to the officer of the watch, Paul Usoko, his Nigerian third officer:

'Bring her round slowly ... port ten. Steer two-four-o.'

The chief moved back to the Engine-Room Consol, while Usoko put the Malayan seaman on the wheel.

'Shift to hand... port ten...'

The master leaned against the wheelhouse central window to watch his ship turning into the wind. He had already knocked her back to ten knots, but he would bring her down further. The hull was designed to take only so much, though she was built throughout with modern, high-tensile steel.

'Slow, both engines...'

Leviathan had begun to swing. The jackstaff on the fo'c'sle-head sixty feet below him was beginning to creep across the last of the disappearing horizon, a horizon that was now an angry line of breaking seas. He still had not become used to this revolutionary design, with the ultra-modern bridge structure, flowing lines sweeping up from the foredeck, perched for'ard in the eyes of the ship. From up here, less than a hundred feet from the stem, the 'dead' distance was reduced to less than an eighth of a mile, the object of positioning the bridge right for'ard, as in the old days. He glanced at the gyro compass card — she was just swinging through north...

She was surprisingly easy to handle, once she had reached five knots; her four rudders, each behind its respective propeller, made her easy to steer; when on passage, the two manoeuvring centre-rudders were locked amidships. Using Shell's ULCC *Batillus*'s pioneering principles, these inclined rudders could be used for an 'emergency stop' — but what the gigantic forces would do to the posts if she was at full speed, was still anyone's guess. The designers had been very reticent during trials...

Leviathan was taking the sea on her port bow... He glanced at the Doppler log displayed next to him, an instrument of uncanny accuracy, able to measure transverse speed fore and aft, in addition to normal ship's speed; she was easing down now; once she had settled she would smash through the seas at about four knots, he reckoned.

'Midships...,' Usoko was ordering. 'Steer two-seven-o.'

Botsaris watched the Nigerian. He, Botsaris, had gone through the traditional seafaring training of most Greek naval reserve officers. Being brought up in the Piraeus, the sea had been his natural calling, but he had got out when the Colonels took over. A few years coasting took him into the Onassis fleet, where he had got stuck on the promotion ladder. A lucky break had taken him into Planeka where he had swiftly climbed to the top, for Kartar Browne liked results, even if his captains did have to cut corners. But these officers, like Usoko, from the emergent nations, these watchkeepers from the states using the flags-of-convenience, how sound were their tickets? Browne did not ask questions, providing his ships were manned and sailed on time — which was why, except for his captains, he was able to pay his officers less than the traditional maritime nations who subscribed to IMCO and worked with the ITWF.

'Course, sir, two-seven-o.'

'Thanks, Paul.'

The Christian name habit had established itself at sea. He did not mind, as long as it did not affect efficiency: life was more relaxed today. The air-conditioning, the enclosed bridges with their comfort; the accommodation concentrated luxuriously into this forward-island complex, reminiscent of a futuristic spaceship, with the crescent-shaped mast curving skywards above the spatial bridge superstructure, all combined to foster this casual approach — that, and the wives who were allowed by most companies to accompany their men. An engineer seldom dirtied his hands; a deckhand rarely went on deck in unpleasant weather. Once the ship was secured for sea, most operations, including the tank-washing and dipping, were remotely controlled from bridge consol positions. The load-on-top principle and the adoption of inert gas tank-filling had eliminated tank explosion dangers. The tiller compartment red blinker was flashing. He picked up the phone; the turboes screamed in the background, as the chief yelled against the fiendish din.

'Number two stopped, Captain. The others are okay.'

'Thanks, Chief. Is it out for the rest of the voyage? D'you want me to get through to the Falmouth agents?'

But the chief had rung off: the racket was intolerable down there. Botsaris strolled towards the starboard door — there would be a slight lee there. He would see how she was taking this weather aft. He picked up his bridge coat and slipped through the door, slamming it shut behind him. He crouched low and scrambled aft, abaft the screen. He would find shelter there, where he could watch the hull stretching abaft him, into the distance...

He stood in the lee of the radio office window, his hands stuffed in his pockets, his collar pulled up to his ears. Though *Leviathan* was still well south, the night was cold, full of flying water and spray. The Panamanian flag was flapping itself to pieces above him, the white sides of the scimitar mast dripping wet and reflecting the sheen from the steaming light. He could just sight the radar aerial rotating in the darkness above him; he peered over the screen and saw the lifeboat, tinged an eerie green by the glow from the starboard light.

The five pedestal floodlights splashed pools of light upon the vast deck stretching aft into the night. The vertebrae of pipelines — crude, firemain and inert gas — ran down the midship line of the ship, the tank branches running athwartships to each tank, like the skeleton of a flatfish. The acres of steel gleamed from the lakes of loose water swilling rhythmically with the roll; the pump manifolds and the cranes reared like oasis mirages; and, right aft and just visible, the stern island gleamed, almost a thousand feet distant.

This was a moment Giorgios Botsaris would not forget. It was difficult to realize that this, the largest ship in the world, had no funnels, was driven by the energy provided by her four natural-circulation nuclear reactor plants. Aft in that gigantic engine-room, the four reactors were silently providing the energy to power this colossal ship who would require no refuelling for six years.

He did not know how long the cores would last, only that once initial criticality had been achieved on acceptance, the infernal contraptions would bubble away with their primeval power until, almost literally, the end of time. Those four reactors, protected within their leaden shields in the sealed nuclear compartments within the main engine-room, were safeguarded against running wild by innumerable automatic safety devices. He, like many port authorities, sensed an uneasiness over the whole business; though he had been only a kid at the time of Hiroshima, *Leviathan*'s engine-room and the terrible events of August 1945 seemed somehow to be linked, albeit psychologically. Was it enough to guarantee the port authorities of the ports into which *Leviathan* sailed that, if anything went wrong, the reactors would scram automatically? Though he had been put through a short course by the Americans, he did not really understand nuclear physics...

He ducked instinctively as a shower of water cascaded across the shimmering, floodlit deck beneath him. The whole hull shuddered from the blow, while the deck, for as far as he could see, swilled with surging sea. She was fully loaded, down to her marks. She was probably better thus than if she had been in ballast, a slab-sided mountain acres high, to be assaulted by each sea that hurtled upon her from out of the night.

She shivered again to another green one — and he sucked in his breath with fear: the whole upper deck was flexing. He watched the corrugation rippling aft, distinctly saw the stern bending before whipping back again — thank God, the designers and builders had produced better steel, high-tensile and able to withstand these colossal stresses and strains...

He cursed aloud as he was reminded of Kartar Browne and his strange parsimony. If only he had invested in the best equipment, instead of economizing on gear, as he had on the Cargo Distribution Simulator. He could have chosen the fully automatic and computerized version, with which the biggest companies equipped their ships: if only *Leviathan* could have enjoyed the same excellence as Shell's *Batillus*, where the *two* second-in-commands, both experienced officers, operated and continually supervised the cargo loading.

By means of a computer, the stresses in each tank were instantly calculated for the relevant loads. The result was recorded by an electronic strobe which presented a visual curve on the display, above which the tank and hull structure stressing must not exceed. If a dangerous situation was developing, the officers were immediately aware of the hazard. They regarded the panel in front of them which displayed visually all the ship's cargo spaces. They then pumped from one tank to another, similar to the trimming in a submarine, until the computer indicated that the stresses were again within safe limits. For them, it was all so easy, with their superbly presented display...

He glanced again at the sobering sight of the upper deck, then turned to fight his way back to the wheelhouse. His ship was not yet into the eye of the storm. He would be thankful when this night was over.

The half-hour before dawn had always been the worst for Giorgios Botsaris, ever since his cadet days. Preventing his drooping lids from fluttering into sleep, even when he was on his feet, was torture ... but with first light, though the wind was still shrieking about them like a malevolent demon, the anxiety of the night was diminished. He took himself out to the starboard wings again, for a true feel of conditions.

He stood close to the front screen, allowing the wind to buffet the steel lip and to sweep over his head, while he stared down at the fo'c'sle-head which seemed so close beneath him. The mammoth windlasses were two huge hummocks on either side of the stump derrick; the links of the cable were so huge that they were clearly visible, even from here. The bollards were salt-encrusted; the white paint was red-streaked with rust beneath the five metre high gunwales.

And as he watched, *Leviathan* climbed majestically upwards, her bows rearing above the horizon as her gigantic hull lunged from one mountainous crest, hovered an instant, then ponderously smashed into the void of the valley below. These Atlantic troughs must be almost a quarter of a mile long, fifty to sixty feet deep — and he held onto the steel lip as the ship shivered from the blow, trembling again throughout her length. The wall of water trundled in a foaming mass into the well beneath the capstans, roared and foamed against the superstructure before dispersing over the side through the scuppers which were inadequate under these conditions. He felt the knot in his guts, a tension he had endured the night long, for no man yet knew whether these steel monsters could withstand the fury which an ocean storm could hurl upon them.

Force 12 — the met. people had been right; when she forged through the eye at 03.40 she had fought hurricane-force winds, so strong that the anemometer had come up against its stop. He had registered the reading with his own eyes: 128 miles per hour, the storm of the century for this area, possibly... The night had been a holocaust of driving spray and roaring foam, the wave-tops taking off in slabs of flying water, a slash of white around the whole horizon which was impossible to distinguish from the sky. The worst must be over, for the anemometer was flickering at just over ninety miles per hour, but a watery sun was trying to escape from behind the array of clouds swirling in from the south-westward.

He glanced aft again, before turning back into the wheelhouse. This formidable ship owed its efficiency and performance more to the advance of electronic remote control than to any other development — even that of her nuclear reactors. It was due to the Telecommand development that the command control could be sited right forward, the best position in his opinion — nothing was as positive as the Mark 1 Eyeball. From this forward bridge, through the Telecommand complexes, the orders to the main engines could be transmitted direct. He could manoeuvre his engines, as if he was handling a runabout powerboat — two levers, one for each side, the two engines each side being coupled up in tandem, for easy ship handling. If the Telecommand failed, a secondary pneumatic system took over; if that went on the blink, the final resort was hydraulic ... a marvel of man's technical achievement, this ship — and he moved back into the warmth of his wheelhouse.

'The anti-collision gear is defective, Captain,' the navigator said, looking up from the grey box of tricks alongside the radars. 'I'm sorry, sir, but it's beyond me, I'm afraid. It keeps on blowing fuses.'

'It's been doubtful since the Cape,' the master said. 'I won't use it, if it's unreliable.'

He had repeatedly asked the owner to appoint an electrical officer to the ship. But 'running costs' were put forward as the reason for such a deficiency — an error of judgment for which they might pay highly one day. This gadget could plot over forty ships at a time, pre-plotting them to present a 'time-ahead' picture. If a potential collision situation existed, an alarm rang and its red light flashed. Even then, in restricted sea-room, the master had to act swiftly: modern speed and the length of ULCCs required instant decision — *Leviathan*'s stern would swing out nearly a third of a mile, even on the closest of her turns.

She had behaved well during the night. Only twice did she fail to come back, after a particularly vicious sea struck her; he had knocked her down to three but she would only maintain steerage way at four knots. He had lost twelve hours and would be unable to make his dawn ETA on Tuesday, 15 March, even if this filth dispersed soon. He might make the evening, and he sensed a pleasurable wickedness at the thought of the landsmen, with their false standards, being forced to wait on the ship they had fought against for so long...

They had bellyached and procrastinated for over a year, whether to allow *Leviathan* and her sister, *Goliath*, into Pencra. The prejudices of the Cornish people had been easy enough to understand, for theirs was a glorious coast; but it was the politicians from all sides who had been the most objectionable. They might understand nuclear physics, but they could never comprehend the new safeties provided by the 'load-on-top', the holding and ballast tanks, and the automatic inert-gas replenishment when a tank was emptying ... and now, with the great day finally arrived, *Leviathan* was to be twelve hours late.

The delay might perhaps emphasize to the shoreside public that the sea always had the last word, however grandiose Man's triumphs.

There was a limit to which a ship of this size could be classed as accident-proof, even with her Safety Monitoring Consols for fire and flooding. With a crew of only twenty-eight-marine labourers who spoke a foreign language (Malaysian was notoriously difficult) and a mixed nationality officer complement of four deck, one radio officer and four engineers — little slack was left in the rope if anything should go wrong. Kartar Browne would be there to greet him at Falmouth and he would buttonhole him again on the subject of an electrical officer; it was difficult to credit that these monsters were running at a loss...

'The guts is going out of the wind, sir.'

The chief officer, drawn with weariness after the long night, had entered through the port door. The ship was plunging less now.

'Bring her back slowly to starboard,' the master ordered. He would pass his new ETA when the Mayday traffic eased.

CHAPTER 10

He had left a message for Jonathan in The Fox and Grapes, downed a beer and was back in the hospital by one-forty. 'Two o'clock,' the sister had said. 'We should know something by then, Mr Krivine.' There was an unnatural quietness about this empty waiting-room — silence, and the smell of ether...

Sally had woken him at three this morning. He had been shocked by the sight of the blood on the green sheets — the bed had been soaked. Their local doctor had driven her to the hospital himself.

Though they would not let him see her, the staff had been good to him... 'You must,' the gentle sister had said, 'be prepared to face up to the fact that she might lose her baby...'

Their doctor had warned her not to drive herself so hard, but she had worked all hours, on top of everything else, to help him establish Hull Cleaning Services. Those first few months had been hectic. Not only did this scorching June see the establishment of Hull Cleaning Services, but the beginning of a new life — their child for whom Sally had longed so much. Deliciously happy, she had suddenly been smitten by the nesting instinct; she hurled herself into transforming what had been a grubby bothy into their snug, sun-drenched, white-washed Fuchsia Cottage. She had been overwhelmed by the wonder of this new life burgeoning within her and she would probably never reach this quality of bliss again. After enduring those sterile years with Ronald, she was floating upon clouds of wonder — while she became engrossed in putting HCS on its feet.

In those first weeks during the spring of the previous year, David had spent all day and most of the midsummer nights licking the little yard into shape. He mended the roof over the slipway; he renewed the leaking water lines; he laid on electric power to the workshop for the welding plant he bought second hand in Falmouth. He was fortunate in finding all the steel and aluminium he needed at a liquidation sale to build his prototype 'crawler'.

But his best luck had been when he bumped into Alf Kelway, his ex-Outside ERA from *Oswald* days. Alf, who was finding difficulty in finding congenial civvy work, had jumped at the chance of joining Hull Cleaning Services, even for a pittance, during its pioneering days. David had left him in charge of the yard, building the prototype 'crawler'. They needed little imagination to name her after the submarine in which David had done his Jimmy's time before going on to his 'perisher' — the commanding officer's qualifying course. So *Oswald* had grown rapidly beneath the skilled hands of Alf Kelway, whilst David occupied himself with winning contracts and finding divers.

It had been difficult: which came first, the chicken or the egg? Again, he had been lucky: Pat Steele came down from Aberdeen to join him, one of the best divers with whom David had worked on the platforms and, later, in submersibles. And all the while Sally had bashed away at the letters, kept the accounts to the satisfaction of Big Brother, the bank manager, whose eagle eye never closed. She had insisted on keeping as late hours as he: they used to drop into each others' arms too exhausted even for loving... She had been whacked even before disaster had struck ... and David Krivine leaned forwards on the waiting-room chair, his shaggy blond head pressed between his hands...

Those first days had been the best. *Oswald* had more than fulfilled her design expectations — for years he had been dreaming of this mechanical underwater vehicle which could crawl across ships' bottoms, and paint, scrub and anti-foul. One man to operate her, that was all: the vehicle had a slight positive buoyancy, high-pressure jets keeping it against the hull and spreading the paint; eventually Hull Cleaning Services would be developing electronically controlled, unmanned crawlers operated from the upper decks of ships.

Then Carrick Crafts, a small, go-ahead firm in Mylor Creek, had become interested. They undertook the construction of the first Type Is, the first two crawlers to be delivered in mid-July. The results on the first coasters had been so satisfactory that David had ordered two more crawlers for September delivery.

During September he had cleaned and 'two-coat' anti-fouled his first small tanker, a clapped-out ship belonging to Planeka Shipping International. The job had taken three days, using the four Type Is and the prototype. His terms had been half-payment on contract, half on completion; the system had been so successful that he placed the order with Carricks for the first two Type IIs. They were more sophisticated and expensive, so that Carrick could accept the contract only with a 33⅓ per cent cash-down deposit on order. Planeka had paid promptly, so the arrangement had worked well. The Type IIs, the *Rainbows*, were delivered in November, just at the right time, because, with his expanding team of divers, he required a constant supply of ships. To pay his divers and the crew of *Pelican* (the old, wooden mother-ship) he needed a steady demand on his books — his sights were on the VLCCs (and eventually the ULCCs) who were beginning to use the new Pencra terminal.

David shifted his weight in the chair; he was getting cramp again. Two-fifteen: the surgeon should be back soon. God, he hoped he would never have to suffer this agony of waiting again; he preferred action — one reason why Hull Cleaning Services was such a satisfaction. He was a better diver than businessman...

Two days previously he had satisfactorily cleaned and anti-fouled his first big 'un ... another Planeka ship, the *Mikindani* of 94,000 tons. Planeka Shipping International, through that fellow Knud Carlsen, the slippery Dane with whom he had crossed swords after the Rotterdam debacle, had proposed new terms: cash for the whole job, the same as Carrick's — 33⅓ per cent deposit with order, the remainder on completion, if David would guarantee to service all the Planeka ships to a fixed programme. David disliked the Planeka set-up, but he could not refuse at this moment.

He accepted the first deposit (the bank manager was breathing down his neck for the loan repayments) and began servicing Planeka's ships. Carlsen seemed satisfied, even hinting that *Leviathan*, PSI's huge nuclear ULCC, would be offered if the Falmouth port authorities authorized the monster to discharge at Pencra. To cope with his spiralling costs, David used Planeka's deposit to start Carrick building three more Type IIs for February delivery. With his total of eight crawlers, he would be able to cover an ULCC in four days, the divers working in shifts.

Work went well through December and January, but he had begun to worry for Sal's health; the clinic was hinting that, for her safety, an early birth might have to be induced. Her doctor forbade her to go to the 'office', as she liked to describe the ramshackle hut they had propped against the rock face at the back of the yard. She yearned for her child; she heeded her medical adviser and remained a patient, expectant mum in Fuchsia Cottage, counting the days and knitting baby clothes … and he remembered wistfully those soft autumn afternoons as she rocked gently in the chair he had unearthed in the Penryn junk shop. The fuchsia bush to the right of the door half-filled the living-room window, but, for some reason, she refused to cut it back until after the baby; and indeed the crimson, the purple and green against the white-washed wall was a delight to the eye when he arrived home after a difficult day…

Carrick had met their delivery dates: by the middle of February the final three crawlers were ready for collection on payment. David's crews were trained and ready. But until Planeka paid their bill for the anti-fouling of *Mikindani* he had no cash with which to pay Carrick — his first charge, the bank's repayments, was due at the end of the month.

He got up as he heard footsteps in the corridor. To hell with Planeka and that mob, though they were causing him extreme stress — and hence the state of anxiety into which Sally had drifted. He could never have been a surgeon — what a fearful load *they* carried — and the state was bludgeoning even the surgeons into line, like regimented dustmen, with all the rest of us — yes, even us divers, the most independent fraternity in the kingdom…

'David…' the thin man in the grey suit was saying. 'They told me in the pub you were here. Is she all right?'

'Johnny…' He had arrived at the right moment. 'Sit down, old lad.'

And so the wait continued: the pace in the hospital warmed up again and the afternoon dragged into evening, the hours punctuated by cups of tea from the nurses. Then they were alone again in the waiting-room.

'So Planeka've got me,' David concluded quietly. 'I've never met that bastard Browne. He does everything through his winger, a chap called Knud Carlsen, who came to see me privately yesterday. He told me that Planeka want me up against the wall, so that Browne can buy out Hull Cleaning Services for his fleet. Carlsen told me in confidence that he, personally, was fed up with Planeka and Kartar Browne. He's leaving the company at the end of next month to take over Marine Maintenance (UK).

'A good outfit?' Jonathan asked wearily. He looked flogged to death.

'Fair enough name in the trade,' David replied. 'They dabble in everything from supply ships for the platforms to bottom cleaning. But Carlsen has something interesting to propose: he wants HCS for himself. He couldn't care less about Browne and will be thankful to be rid of him. That Dane may be a slimy one, Johnny, but he's not a mean bastard like his lord and master.'

His twin brother raised his eyebrows, but said nothing. David continued:

'Knud is offering to buy Hull Cleaning Services for £20,000 plus stock at valuation. He'll continue trading under its name. He'll pay me £8,000 a year to go on running it, plus a bonus of £5,000 in cash if I promise to keep my mouth shut. He doesn't want Browne to know anything about the deal.'

'Take it, Dave,' Jonathan said. 'You've no choice, if what you say is true about Browne, who's got you where he wants you. If you don't accept Carlsen's offer — a generous one in my opinion — Browne will bankrupt you.'

'I'd do anything to foul-up Browne,' David said. 'Twice he's played me a dirty trick; I'm not sure he either knows or cares that I'm the same bloke who got his ship away from Rotterdam.'

Jonathan snorted. David was amused by this new Jonathan, this city gent with the immaculate suiting, black box-type briefcase, rolled umbrella even in darkest Cornwall. ''Course he knows,' Mr Jonathan Krivine said. 'Kartar Browne is one of the slickest operators in the shipping business; he's got his way in the end with his nuclear ships. His *Leviathan*'s due in this evening, isn't she? The Pencra authorities had to give in; the ecologist lobby hasn't a chance against international finance. Grow up, David.'

David felt his hackles rising. This man from Lloyd's was a stranger. Jonathan used to care, once … but he had given up. He had never bothered, as David had, to fight the pollution octopus. Jonathan had never witnessed a blow-out — and the image of Essofisk during the late seventies, its black filth fouling miles of the North Sea for days on end, swept vividly into David's imagination.

David was staring down the corridor when a door opened. Two white-coated figures emerged in close consultation, the taller shaking his head as he slowly crossed to the other side of the wide room. The other, David could recognize now, was the sister. She caught his glance and began walking briskly towards him.

'How is she?' David asked.

The woman gently took his arm. 'Come with me, Mr Krivine,' she said, glancing briefly towards Jonathan. 'Mr Cairns will see you now.'

Jonathan had never before seen his twin brother like this: a terrible rage was seething inside him. David had refused to speak after the sister had brought him back from the gynaecologist's room. 'Drive me to Manacle Point,' was all that he said. 'I want to see *his* ship.'

So Jonathan had driven the Ford out to Gweek before turning back to Porthoustock where they left the car. They walked up to the cliff edge together, where they stood gazing down upon the ocean, a grey sea this evening, cold and drear. The swell was surging across the Manacles below them, the rocks dark against the curl of breaking waves. To the northward, St Anthony Head seemed so close in this visibility that he could almost touch it, where the coastline merged, green, red and distant blue, into Gerrans Bay behind; and to the southward, past Black Head, the Western Channel stretched to the horizon, hazy and mysterious, towards Land's End and the Atlantic.

'There she is,' he said softly. 'Coming up over the horizon now.' He pointed to the strange white dome, floating above the horizon line. 'Odd, isn't she, Dave, without funnels?'

But still his brother remained silent, his blue eyes brittle. The gulls mewed and wheeled above the causeway stretching from the shore to the southern breakwater of the Pencra terminal. A gap separated the second mole which, over a mile long, ran northwards for the tankers who were already using the haven.

'*Leviathan* will take the northern buoy, I suppose, Dave?'

David whipped round, grabbed Jonathan's upper arms in his ham hands:

'The doc said he may have to take the baby away. He's giving it another month. "It's Mrs Grant or the child," he said.'

Those blue eyes were burning with hate, mad almost...

'What's the real cause?' Jonathan asked gently. 'Did he tell you that?'

'Shock,' David said, shaking his huge head. 'The doctor puts it down to last week's news. Thanks to Browne, we're bankrupt — after all we've tried to do.'

Then suddenly he was calm. He spoke softly, his speech controlled, his face drained of colour.

'I'll kill him, Johnny. I'll throttle him with these hands of mine, if her child is taken from her. Kartar Browne will have murdered it, just as I'll kill him...' His words, spoken softly on the cliff top, floated away on the wind.

Jonathan shivered. Taking his brother's arm, he led him down the cliff-track and back to the car.

CHAPTER 11

She did not usually lose any sleep over him ... but tonight Usha had remained awake for Kartar's return from Cornwall; his affairs in Falmouth had kept him a day longer than he had planned. After her solitary dinner tray, which Deirdre had brought into the drawing-room, she had listened for over three hours to her favourite records — the reproduction from the stereo that Kartar had installed was so excellent that the orchestras seemed to fill the house. As usual, Wagner had stirred her mercilessly; Kartar might even be in one of his rare moods...

The authorities had at last given permission for his new ship to discharge at the Pencra terminal; *Leviathan* had been delayed by the weather and Kartar had to wait twelve hours before going on board. He had rung after dinner. He had dined with some representative from Lloyd's: Kartar had been considering reinsuring this year with the British. He was always one jump ahead. She usually understood him but he had sounded very tense over the phone, even suggesting that she should wait up for him. She felt like a coy bride as she had stepped from her perfumed bath. He rarely dropped such a hint — and she felt both exhilarated and amused.

It was past two when she heard the gravel churning in the drive. She put down her novel — something about the British in India — and slipped into her housecoat. If this did not rouse the male in him, nothing ever would. She had bought the flimsy thing in Harrods; she could still see the amused approbation of the young assistant who had modelled it. To her generation, sex stopped at forty ... and, as far as the

Brownes were concerned, the arrogant puss had been disconcertingly accurate.

Usha reached the front door just as he stepped in from the darkness. A covering of frost was whitening the steps, and she shivered as she closed the door behind him. She bent towards him, surprised when he responded to her lips.

'I've a thermos of milk,' she said. 'Would you like it in bed?'

She climbed the stairs slowly, while he followed her, moaning about the day. 'I'm getting old,' he said. 'Fed up with stupidity and inefficiency.'

He had stripped off and came directly to her bed. He lay alongside her, his arms cradled beneath his head, staring at the ceiling. 'I'm tired, Usha, more tired than I've ever been in my life.'

She listened to his voice, a monologue of the last two days, but she did not take in his words. She was deprived, she supposed, for why else should she want this stocky little man? She still had her pride; she would wait for him. He might even stop talking for a moment... Mechanical it might be, but that was better than nothing.

'Usha, you're not listening.'

'Thinking about us.'

He ignored her remark and continued: 'I don't want your advice normally, but I need your brain tonight. I'm worried like hell. The ULCCs are making fearful losses, Usha.'

'You told me that it would be like this for a while,' she said. 'Worse than you expected?'

'The recession on the crude market has gone on too long,' and then he almost shouted the words: '*I've built the wrong type of ship*. We need versatile ships now, able to switch cargoes, enter estuaries. The tanks in the ULCCs are built to take only crude.

Under present conditions, *Leviathan* and *Goliath* are losing me big money every day. They're killing Planeka.'

She slipped her arm beneath his shoulders, and drew his head to her breast.

'You're worn out,' she whispered. 'Can't you forget business for tonight? You'll be better in the morning.' He did not resist, even when she pressed herself closely to him.

'I called in at the office on my way through,' he murmured. 'There was an urgent note from the secretary. The Inland Revenue are really gunning for me now. We'll have to get out at the end of the year, Usha.'

She remained silent: this acknowledgment of defeat was so unlike him. For years he had learned to live with the tax people. Always a jump ahead, tax avoidance was a sport he enjoyed.

'My dear,' she whispered. 'Forget it all tonight.' Her hands wandered, caressing him, waiting for his response. In their early days, he would not have taken as long as this...

'It's one blow after another, Usha. Carlsen gave me the result of the initial scrubbing survey...'

She gently took him, felt his automatic response, knew that he would come as soon as she beckoned. 'Yes?' she murmured.

He remained rigid alongside her, in spite of himself.

'That was bad enough — but Lloyd's won't give automatic cover. I've got to wait until she turns round again at Kharg Island. They're even inflicting one of their men on me for a round trip in her.'

'That's not so bad, is it, darling? So long as you get the cover...'

She could see the great ship in her imagination: she had named it in the American dock ... a huge monstrous barge that would carry millions of barrels of crude oil across one side of the world to the other — to fill the Browne coffers? Not even for their children, for they were childless, barren of the love and tenderness which should exist between a man and his woman... 'Oh God,' she breathed, 'my God' ... and suddenly she thrust him from her, repelled by this callous, dead creature; he thought of himself as a captain of industry, a financial wizard controlling world events. But a *man*, a lover who could make his woman happy? Kartar Browne had never tried, in spite of her coaxing, her patient understanding over these long years. He had not even sensed that she had withdrawn to her side of the bed...

'I met Knud today,' he was continuing. 'A competent guy — and a smooth operator. It's a good thing every man has his price, Usha.' Then suddenly he turned towards her, his hands groping. He laughed, his words like dirty slops. 'And every woman too, eh, my Usha?'

She shut off her mind, deliberately provoking the passion flickering within her. She yielded to his grossness, wringing the last spasm of pleasure from his lust. As he flung himself from her, he snapped off the light.

'You're my wife, Usha,' he said softly. 'You're in this with me — right to the bloody end.'

CHAPTER 12

'Yes, Mr Carlsen, come down at once. We can't work on *Leviathan* today, anyway. The unions are blacklisting her, now they realize whose ship she is — a token affair which shouldn't last long. Don't forget to bring the plans. Yes, I'll meet you.' David had hung up; he could catch up on his paperwork during what was left of the morning. He drove to Truro after a snack lunch and met the one-forty-five. Knud Carlsen was all smiles as he stepped from his first-class compartment.

'Better circumstances, this time, eh, Mr Krivine?' He took both David's hands in his, an Americanism which David detested. 'Call me Knud,' he beamed.

'I'm David.'

So they had driven down to Trefusis. The overweight man in the light raincoat stood for a moment, admiring Fuchsia Cottage. 'Say, it's a real gem, David.' His round face creased benevolently, as he had allowed himself to be ushered inside.

'Sally's in hospital,' David said. 'We won't be interrupted here. I don't know whether Mr Browne's still in the ship.'

'Makes sense.' Carlsen snapped open his briefcase. 'I've had my lawyers check the contract. They'll send the papers down as soon as they've completed things.' The Dane looked up, his eyes radiating good humour. 'I take it you're willing to start at once. You're the managing director of Hull Services now — better than the worries of being the proprietor, eh?' and he clapped David across the shoulders. 'Marine Maintenance is proud to own its subsidiary — and the Planeka contract should give us years of work.' He looked up and David caught the glint of satisfaction in his eyes. 'Sure you're happy with the salary?'

David nodded. 'Eight thousand is a generous start,' he said. 'I won't be greedy until we see how it goes.'

'Sure — don't want to kill the goose...' Carlsen guffawed as he produced his pen. 'I'll sign first.' He pushed the contract towards David.

'Use my pen...'

So that was it; David could begin tomorrow, 18 March. The mother-ship, his old wooden trawler, *Pelican*, was ready, the eight crawlers stowed in the welldeck.

'I can start at dawn. We have to skim *Leviathan*'s sides first, before she lightens. We'll finish her in four days, if there are no snags.'

'A preparatory scrub for your survey, that's what you suggest?'

'We can give her a thorough scrub at Kharg Island. She'll have only twenty-eight days' growth when she gets back to Pencra again. A light going-over, then we can anti-foul her.'

Carlsen was unrolling sheaves of *Leviathan*'s line drawings across the kitchen table.

'1,475 feet long, 226 feet beam, 104 feet draught — four days for a pass?' Carlsen whistled softly as he glanced at David. 'Sure?'

'Barring snags. We work in shifts down the fore-and-aft line; we can do half the flats in a day. *Pelican* keeps pace with the crawlers who work in line abreast. We start aft, so the stream keeps the muck clear: the drivers can see where they are going. I usually follow later, on our prototype crawler, so see that all's well.'

'I can depend on you being able to anti-foul *Leviathan* on her next call here?'

'Certainly — and we can almost rely on strike action these days, to give us extra time. It helps if we can do her at full working load, because her sides remain wet. These modern paints have changed things.'

Carlsen had spread the designs of her bottom across the table. He produced a chit from his wallet briefcase, then carefully identified seven points across the ship's 'flats'.

'Here, at the junction of the transverse bulkhead of C main cargo tank and the side tanks, Y3 and Y4. And here, David, across the main midship tank, D main cargo, at D15 and DI6.' He pored across the plan, located what he was seeking: '... and here, at G main cargo, junction of G25 and G26. I'll circle them in red.' He glanced up, scrutinizing, probing... 'These are exact positions on her bottom. I want you to scrub these points very carefully, then mark them off with radioactive paint so that you'll be able to locate them easily again when the ship gets back here. You've got to be accurate.'

'I'll do the job myself. I use the keel as my datum for our measurements. That's how HCS achieves precision, Knud. My team knows it has to be accurate or else...' He glanced across the table to where Carlsen was marking off another cross.

'What d'you want these patches for, Knud?'

The Dane looked up, a patronizing smile creasing his volatile face. 'I'm looking ahead a bit, Dave. You know Kartar Browne's itching to get hold of a set-up such as yours — ours — to clean his ships himself?'

David grinned. 'He's got a job on, now that Marine Maintenance has collared the South West. Does he know you're behind MM?'

Carlsen grimaced. 'No. That's why I'm retaining the name of HCS. My contract with Planeka doesn't run out until the end of next month.'

'Another six weeks to go, then. Tricky, isn't it?'

'I'm keeping out of Kartar's way as much as I can. My relief has already taken over as operations manager. I'll be bloody glad, though, to be finished with Browne. He's a right bastard.'

'You'll give me all the administrative help you can to get my eight crawlers out to the Gulf? Unless you do, I can't keep to your programme.'

'You'll have Marine Maintenance behind you.'

David shrank from Carlsen's reassuring clasp — but he had to work with him now. 'We've had to work fast, you and I,' Knud was continuing. 'My capital has paid Carrick so that you can get your full team of eight crawlers to work. I'm glad you've joined me, David, real glad. We've got years of work between us. You have the diving know-how...'

'You've got the business sense,' David answered, hating himself. 'But why do you want me to mark off these rectangles? I'm intrigued.'

'Confidential. Don't breathe a word about this — not even to your friends. Give me your word, David? K.B. has his industrial spies everywhere. I'll make it worth your while, boy, I promise you.'

'Okay. But what's it all about?'

Carlsen was hesitating, his pale blue eyes still wary. He lowered his voice, lit a cigar as he dropped into the kitchen chair: 'In the States last year, I ran across a bright boy. He was researching marine growth for one of their largest paint firms. As well as being a chemist, he's a successful electronics engineer; he was perfecting an underwater device which would monitor the growth of marine weed under different speeds, temperatures and conditions. He was looking for ships to accept his device for trial purposes. *Leviathan* is his first nuclear ULCC. He's offering us the results, free, if he can use

Leviathan. If we can match up the right composition for our anti-fouling paint, we can outstrip our competitors by years. Our service could save Browne millions.' Carlsen was nearer to being excited than David had ever seen him. 'If *we* can use the monitoring results before anyone else nobbles them, we'll collar the market.'

'And Browne will be forced to pay our prices.' David was grinning. 'You're taking it on?'

'Nothing to lose. That's why you've got to mark off these patches *now.* I'll have the pods ready for you to fit when *Leviathan* gets back to Pencra.'

Carlsen pushed the plans across the table. 'They're copies of the originals. Remember, I'm officially still working for Planeka for another six weeks.'

Cunning sod, David thought. *If he can do this to Browne behind his back, what are my chances?* But he had landed this job now — and the money was good: 'I'll start at dawn.' He smiled briefly. 'Thanks, Knud. It's a relief to have real backing behind me. Hull Cleaning Services will be world-wide soon.' He raised his tumbler as he poured the Dane another scotch.

'Skol…' Carlsen clasped David's hand again. 'Just between the two of us, remember. I'll make it worth your while.' He rose ponderously. 'Can you get me back to Truro? Drive by the coast, if you like. I'd like to see your ship.'

His crews were huddled on the jetty in the half-light of dawn. The launch was waiting at the steps.

'All set?' he asked the small man who detached himself from the group.

'All here,' Alf Kelway said. 'Pat Steele ain't so hot, sir. Birthday yesterday.'

They surged out of Falmouth harbour, left the blockhouse gaunt above them against the lightening sky. The blue lights on the breakwaters were flickering in the bay and soon the silhouette of the ship seemed on top of them, she was so gigantic. Twenty minutes later, David was leaning across *Pelican*'s bridge rail, watching his divers donning their heated suits.

Under Alf's leadership, even the most difficult characters had begun to toe the line: discipline was all-important in this underwater business. The secret lay in keeping station on each other as the eight crawlers moved slightly forwards, in line abreast across these vast bottoms.

There was one essential David always carried out himself. He always went down first, taking Alf as his driver, to mark off the datum line with white radioactive paint. They used *Oswald* who, in spite of her relative age, was still good enough for such elementary tasks.

With a vessel of *Leviathan*'s proportions, the vertical sides had to be scrubbed first, a longer job than cleaning the flat bottom surface, because the crawler team had to change over every 240-feet-wide sweep, each vehicle covering thirty feet. *Pelican* worked forwards with them, tending their lines as they progressed.

They would complete the port vertical side today, the starboard side tomorrow. They could start on the port half of the bottom on Sunday; by the evening of Monday 21 March, the job could be finished.

So much depended on the drill being carried out meticulously, particularly blowing-through and cleaning the gear afterwards. Hull Cleaning Services succeeded because the technique was simplified to its utmost, *Pelican* bearing the brunt of the heavy work. The drill had been perfected, they had done it so often now.

When working on the 'flats' the crawlers lined up athwartships, starting aft. The drivers used the inboard crawler as their 'flagship', keeping station on her as she moved towards the bow at just over three feet per minute. The scrubber attachments, like the paint sprayers, covered thirty feet overall, so eight crawlers had an overlap, the 'admiral' having a yard's play as he drove along the centre-line. The scrubbers, the latter being eighteen nylon-bristled, revolving brushes actuated by compressed air, were arrayed well behind the machines. Because the ship was at anchor or swinging to her buoy, she would always be lying to the wind or stream, which saved the drivers from being blinded by the clouds of dirt or paint mist.

As David watched the last crawler being hoisted over the side by the trawl boom (*Pelican* was an old side-winder), he remembered the days and nights he worked the submersibles. During bad weather, waiting for conditions to moderate, he had whiled away the time by designing the perfect 'crawler', an underwater painting vehicle, or UPV as it became known.

The difficulty had always been propulsion, and the provision of a sufficient supply of paint; he had solved the former problem by reducing the friction between crawler and ship's bottom to a minimum. By using the same principle as in submersibles — the admission of oil into a sphere to provide more buoyancy — the driver could finely tune his vehicle to a slight positive buoyancy, just enough for adhesion between the driving wheels and the ship's bottom plates.

The latter problem of paint supply had been resolved by eradicating altogether the paint reservoir on the UPV, a system with two disadvantages: the paint soon ran out and it took time to resurface and recharge the paint reservoirs. In David's system, the mother-ship provided unlimited paint by forced supply from her own tanks. *Pelican* stocked enough paint for a four-day operation, with eight crawlers working.

Above all else, by working two-hour shifts, the divers could remain at depth — an enormous advantage when working the bottoms of these deep-draught ships: UPV operators could be working up to 120 feet when *Leviathan* was fully laden, when eight crawlers could cover a half flat in a day. A one-coat anti-fouling would take four days, instead of nearly as many weeks in a costly dry dock — and there were too few of these around the world.

'Ready, Alf?' he shouted down to the welldeck.

Kelway shook his head — number seven had a leak in one of its pressure joints.

Oswald was being slung over the side; while the others were catching their trim, he and Alf would run down the centre-line. It was lucky that he had had these months in which to perfect his techniques — and he surreptitiously touched the wooden rail on which he was leaning — no accidents so far. He had insisted on *Pelican* having on board the necessary decompression chamber and all the gear. In emergency, he could whistle up the doc who was always on call at Falmouth through VHF.

He had too many memories of the unpredictable effects from diving accidents at depth — and even from the shallower levels, if the medical team was not instantly available: the tragedy of Bert Strang was still too poignant. The medicos knew now that Bert was doomed for life from the effects of his injuries, though these had not been due to bad decompression: Bert and he had not been under pressure in *Seaveyor*. But after that tragedy, David had made it his business to study the physiological problems affecting divers at depth

— instinctively he glanced at the after superstructure where the decompression unit was housed. He prayed daily that he would never have to use it in an emergency. The effects of the three various forms of the 'bends' were caused, it was thought, by the escape of nitrogen from the bloodstream when the body was under pressure, a state of affairs obtaining when divers were working 'free' as were his men.

David Krivine strolled aft to the after deck house where *Pelican*'s diesel generators were pounding away, providing the electrical power for the motors and compressors. His last check before diving was to see that the bottles were fully charged and the compressors at immediate notice... Arthur Tregent, skipper of *Pelican*, was chatting with his mechanic by the port quarter.

'We're nice and snug, David,' Tregent shouted. 'I'm ready to warp when you are.'

David joined them at the rail beneath *Leviathan*'s starboard quarter. The ship had swung to the ebb; dew was glistening on her orange plates as the first light stole up from below the horizon. This was a big day in Hull Cleaning Services' history; a pity he had to be doing the job for a shipowner who was a two-timing bastard: the Rotterdam incident was still too recent, as also the dubious blackmailing methods when trying to buy out HCS.

Alf was carefully bearing off *Oswald* who was being slung over the side. He was one of the best divers David had encountered — a careful man, navy trained, too experienced to take chances. He had once suffered a touch of the 'niggles'. He had never again been careless.

The mildest of the three types of 'bends' were the 'niggles'. They were the first indication to the doctor and the decompression team parties that things were not as they should be — the diver did not feel right, was not suffering pain in any of his muscle blocks, but usually in the stomach. His back could be painful, and also his leg and chest muscles. Alf had been hauled up too quickly after experiencing trouble at depth. He was lucky not to have suffered type two bends which were the killer...

A man who was hauled up from depth too quickly and who was not decompressed in time would almost certainly suffer from type two bends: these manifestations were of severe illness, and with pain that could be equated with the agony suffered by a stomach-ulcer patient. The pain could be anywhere: severe headaches, vomiting, extremely painful and severe chest pains, like those of a coronary sufferer. The diver looked terrible, sweating and often becoming unconscious. He appeared shocked and could have severe abdominal pains at the same time. All these symptoms were thought to be caused by the liberation of nitrogen bubbles into the chest and the abdomen; and, if into the brain, he would lose consciousness — if he was not immediately decompressed to the original deep pressures, or even higher, the man would certainly die.

Very often, a man with severe type two bends looked as if he had experienced a stroke — and David tried to obliterate his memories of men who had been damaged for life: they could be damaged down one side, their faces 'gone', mouth drooping on one side, an eye that would not close — the symptoms were identical to those of a coronary ... and these effects could occur twenty-four hours after decompression, though they usually appeared about six hours afterwards. If a man surfaced at four o'clock, his symptoms would begin showing before midnight — and horrible they were, bringing the terrors of impending death.

David threw the two switches, watched the pointers flickering on the compressor gauges ... the only possible remedy for type two bends was to recompress the diver immediately. With luck, all the symptoms would disappear, and then he would have to decompress very carefully and slowly, perhaps over a period lasting three days. Recompression was the golden rule, by medical men, if possible, as was now being practised at Aberdeen. Here at Falmouth, David had arranged for the recompression lock to be alongside the work — in the after deckhouse of *Pelican*.

The most sinister of the bends were those about which the least was known, type three. In these cases, X-rays showed changes in the bone structure, but the first signs might not become apparent for as long as twelve months after exposure to breathing the compressed air. Pain might be felt two years afterwards, and within five years the diver would be crippled.

He glanced up once more at the great ship. She was already unloaded, but her plating showed rust marks and her sides were encrusted white with salt. She had caught a dusting in the bay, catching the tail-end of the Force 12 which had swept up from the Azores a few days ago. Her draught marks here were showing sixteen metres. If the strike had only continued for another day or so, he would not have been so pushed for time... Checking his suit he began to move forward to join Alf.

'Okay, Arty — normal drill.' He pulled down his facemask and rolled backwards over the side.

They completed the port side on Friday; at 18.30, Saturday, on schedule, they finished the starboard side and the rudders. At dawn on Sunday, 20 March, they began their first run along the port flat of *Leviathan*'s bottom.

With Alf at the controls, *Oswald* waited, well ahead and on the centre-line, for the eight crawlers to sort themselves out. David, in *Oswald*'s co-driver's seat, was impatiently watching the wavering lights. What were they waiting for? The 'admiral' had only to follow Alf's Glo-line up the keel-line. David grunted inside his facemask as he saw them move slowly forward, their whirring scrubbers churning off the muck behind them. *Oswald* would soon reach the bulbous bow. They could then cross to the starboard side and run down to the stern. He and Alf could then work up the starboard side, measuring off and scraping the patches which Carlsen had demanded. By the time *Oswald* had finished the starboard side, the crawlers would be well up the port section, so Alf and he could mark off the port side. There were only six patches in all, on the starboard side, excluding the three tricky ones by the condensers and the reactor circulator inlets: these could only be finished with the ship's co-operation.

Alf was driving. The darkness down here was complete, except for the blurred beam thrown out by the powerful lamps which David was controlling. The measuring had taken time, but had been easier than they had expected, thanks to Alf's marked lines which he had painted on the ship's sides. David had checked from these datums and, by measuring from the hull openings marked on the plan, he was certain of his accuracy. He would check them after the dinner break. They completed the starboard side, crossed over to the port at the stern, then moved forward at full speed to catch up with the 'admiral'. The driver held up his thumb and pointed upwards. The shifts needed a break in the diving bells, before finishing off the afternoon scrubbing. They couldn't start 'bleeding' (the low decompression process on their way to the surface) much before teatime.

They wasted no time — food, water and a short rest whilst they chiakked together — and then they were again manoeuvring their crawlers. Alf reckoned there remained only a third left to finish. David dipped below the airlock and rejoined *Oswald*; Alf sheered her away from the scrubbers which were already moving off on their final run.

Oswald steadied nicely, Alf steering her across to the intake opening. David re-checked from the ballast pump suction. Alf applied the single scrubber, David finishing the patch off by hand with a wire brush; then onto D14, but, by then, the crawlers were tangling around the bow. Alf grinned at David as *Oswald*'s scrubber dabbed again at the patch which David had just cleaned: the language must be choice up in the fore-ends.

David gave the patch a final brush. His lamp gleamed on the old paint, a dull brick red after the cleaning, the sediment from his work spiralling astern as a red wisp. He moved closer to the steel to inspect the thoroughness of the crawlers' work. The bottom had badly needed a going-over; in sections the weed was over six inches long.

They had done well today. The plates, welded in neat lines, stretched into the gloom, rough but clean — and then he noticed a rift in the anti-fouling, straighter than the lamination which old anti-fouling often assumed. He swam close to it, his legs working steadily in the stream. There was a definite cracking in the paint which ran away from him, in a straight line transversely across the bottom. Alf turned *Oswald* and followed David who was groping across the hull and following the slender line. They reached the starboard side, the paint crack slanting aft, close to position D15 which they had previously scraped. Alf would have noticed nothing, as he was intent on steering *Oswald* to David's signals.

Perhaps this hairline was normal, merely the usual hull-whip experienced by tankers? He would say nothing to Alf. They would finish checking the starboard side and they could then start 'bleeding' for surfacing. When he returned to Fuchsia Cottage, he would tell Carlsen confidentially about the hairline. He hoped he would be back home on Sunday night.

CHAPTER 13

She felt strong enough by the morning of 22 March to accompany David down to the cliffs overlooking the Manacles. She insisted on leaving the car and together they slowly climbed the sheep track to the top. Bowed against the wind, she shook her hair and stood with him to watch his first ULCC sailing from the Pencra terminal.

'I feel proud. Few men would have got over all the snags and finished her in time,' she murmured. 'I like being seen with you in Falmouth,' and she pressed his hand. 'You've done well in a year, David.'

'We can thank the strike for the extra time,' he said brusquely. 'She looks good, even in ballast. Not bad that red on her sides, is it?' and they laughed together there in the buffeting wind. White horses were speckling the bay and the seas, breaking white over the Manacles outcrop, were surging against the gigantic new breakwaters.

'They knew what they were doing when they built Pencra,' he said. 'The gap between the moles allows the stream to flow naturally, without causing too much back-eddy, particularly at springs.'

The great ship was turning in a full half-circle, her rudders kicking up a wash as she worked up to half power. 'She'll steer south-east until she's eight miles east of Black Head. Then she'll alter to the southward to cross the separation zone at right angles. She has to follow this recommended route, if she wants to use Pencra. She won't alter up for the deep water off Ushant, until she's five miles south of the east-bound traffic route. At last, IMCO is being heeded throughout the world.

Even Browne has to conform now, if he wants to use the world's facilities.'

She enjoyed listening to him. The sea was his life, something he understood better than the casuistry of the business world. His long hair was ruffled by the wind; he was pale from overwork, but the strain that was showing two days ago when she left the hospital was diminishing.

They did not mention the baby. The doctors were allowing her to keep it, but they both knew the risk she was taking. This was their last chance: 'Oh, God,' she whispered to herself, as she had done so often during these last days, 'bless our child.' She closed her eyes, clung to him as she entwined her arms through his. Theirs was the real world, the miracle of creation … she supposed many mothers-to-be felt similarly at this stage. It was difficult, facing the mystery of evolving life inside her, not to feel close to her God.

'My David,' she whispered. 'I wish you didn't have to leave me just now.'

He tilted up her chin to kiss her lightly on the lips.

'You know I've got to go. Our future depends on my making a good job of this first ULCC. Look at her out there — a picture of functional power. With no funnel, she's hideous, isn't she? The big 'uns will never be the same again after these two.'

'How long will you be in Kuwait? When will you be back?'

'I'll fly out with the gear and the crews. It'll take a week or two to modify the diving boat which we're hiring. We've got to be ready for *Leviathan* when she arrives,' and he nodded to seaward, where the tanker was almost hull down… 'Twenty-six days from here… I've booked an air passage back on twenty-seventh April. I'll be leaving Alf to get the crews and the gear back. It's the twenty-second of March today, so I'm bound to be away for five weeks, Sal.'

His eyes were troubled as he gazed down at her: 'Carlsen said he was raising more capital. He's forming a similar outfit in the Gulf — he's calling the subsidiary, Hull Cleaning Services (Kuwait) Ltd. Then I'll be able to operate at either end — it will save this expensive performance of flying out the gear. But there has to be a first time — if it's a success, Carlsen won't hesitate to set up the Kuwait subsidiary.' His arm tightened about her. 'It's for us both, my Sal,' he said quietly, his words barely audible against the wind. 'For the three of us...'

Tears were very close. She could have been so utterly at peace up here, staring down at the rocks where the seas surged. The gulls wheeled upon the air currents, screaming and squabbling where they nested amongst the tufts of seapinks. The clouds were sweeping majestically up-channel, like the galleons of Spain centuries ago — and in her emotional state she could almost see them, the floating fortresses, pendants flaunting the Spanish arms, whilst Drake's ships were slipping their cables in Plymouth Sound...

'Alf Kelway will be flying out with the crews,' he was saying. 'They'll need a few days to acclimatize. I'm glad you suggested making him my second-in-command; I don't know what I'd do without him.'

'It's all happened so quickly, David. I wish I could go on helping while you're away, but the doctor says I'll be all right if I don't do too much.' Her eyes misted again. The baby was due in May, even if it went full-term. If only she had parents to whom she could go...

'You're to call me direct, if you need me urgently,' he said. 'I can be back within twenty-four hours.'

'How would I get in touch?'

'Through Carlsen. He's on telex direct to the Gulf.'

'I don't trust him,' she said.

'You've never met him.'

'Woman's instinct. You've told me enough about him.'

'He's all right, now that he's cutting adrift from Planeka.'

She did not reply. David had enough worries already. She leaned against him as he watched *Leviathan* merging with the horizon.

'Carlsen's a phlegmatic Dane all right,' David said. 'Nothing excites him, except the mention of his present boss.'

'He's leaving Browne, you said, at the end of next month.'

'Another six weeks. I assume he's still loyal, for *Leviathan*'s sake.'

Then he told her of the hairline he had found in the anti-fouling paint. 'I informed Carlsen. He said he would report the findings to Kartar Browne. Carlsen rang me the next day, not at all concerned — "It's up to the owner," he said, "to take the vital decisions."' The ULCC had suffered enough delay already with the strike. Even at anchor, her daily running costs were astronomical.

'They can't be too worried,' she said. She was feeling the chill but they lingered, watching the vanishing ship, whose cupola-shaped bridge was still just visible.

'He's an intelligent guy, Carlsen. He's fitting monitors to *Leviathan*'s bottom. I've got to scrape off more patches along the hairline. I wish he'd told me before.'

'You can do them at Kharg Island, can't you, David?'

'That's what I'll do. He wants to see if there are any chemical changes in the anti-fouling where I found the hairline. Just one more thing — camel's back... Carlsen was secretive about it all — I was to tell no one...'

As they walked back along the cliff path, she could see another tanker weighing anchor inside the Pencra haven. She would be moving onto the terminal buoy which *Leviathan* had vacated. Tugs were fussing around her and, above the wind, she caught the sound of their hooters. The terminal had come into its own just in time, now that the oil was on stream from the Celtic fields. She tossed back her head, feeling the wind in her hair. She wondered when they would be together again up here, sharing the scenery of Falmouth Bay and the Helford estuary which they loved so much.

'Sal...'

'Yes?'

'Carlsen offered me £5,000 in cash to keep my mouth shut.' He was drawing apart from her.

'Did you accept, David?'

''Course I did, with the manager clamouring for this month's instalment.'

'I wish you hadn't.'

'Why?'

'Puts you under an obligation.'

They walked on in silence until they regained the car. He was holding open the door for her. 'Why did Carlsen want to do that?' He was talking aloud: 'Why, Sal?'

He slammed the door. He did not speak again until they reached the cottage.

CHAPTER 14

Captain Botsaris, twenty-two years at sea and seven of them in command of tankers, always felt a prick of excitement as he entered the Persian Gulf.

'It's true what they say about the east, Jonathan,' he said to the Englishman. 'The mystery starts east of Suez. It's a pity we have to come round by the Cape.'

They were on Christian name terms. He, Giorgios, had been apprehensive at being burdened for the whole voyage by the Lloyd's representative, but the fellow had been easy enough. Krivine asked intelligent questions and Giorgios had given him the free run of the ship. The crew reported well of him and, by all accounts, Jonathan seemed satisfied with *Leviathan* and how she was run — not that the latter was any part of his business, but Lloyd's would not insure at a viable rate if the ship was a shambles...

The two men were standing in the starboard wings of the bridge structure — it was good to feel the breeze out here. The length of the upper deck stretched away abaft them, the central vertebrae of inert gas and oil lines running to the after island. The air shimmered above the vents which sprouted like mushrooms between the transverse spurs connecting the tanks to the main lines. The helicopter pad on the port side was the only space in this maze of pipes.

'Once Ras Masandam is astern, I always feel the trip's over,' Botsaris said. 'We should be at the terminal buoy by tomorrow evening.'

'To think that this was once the navy's punishment station for its failures,' Krivine said. 'And now it's the world's treasure house.'

'The Persian Gulf,' Giorgios said, 'there're as many dollars here as grains of sand.'

'The oil will run out one day. An interesting day for the planet.'

'How much longer do you need before making your report, Jonathan? I've just received a telex ordering me not to sail on the return voyage until I have definite information on the insurance cover. It depends on you, Jonathan.' The master grinned as he caught Krivine's eye. He had not intended to prod the Englishman, but the captain of the ship had the right to know what was going on.

'I'll report as soon as I've seen the agent, Captain.' Krivine was smiling bleakly; he was a close one.

The day dragged on, the land hazy to the northward as *Leviathan* ploughed up the Gulf at her unladen speed of eighteen knots, the islands of Farur and Shaikh Shu'aib coming abeam during the evening. The merciful arrival of twilight enveloped the pulsing ship as, to port, outward-bound tankers streamed in endless procession, their lights twinkling in the dust-laden air. Captain Botsaris spent the night in his clothes; there were too many idiots at sea these days. He was master of the largest ship in the world and he refused to be labelled with the stigma that all ships wearing the flags of convenience were necessarily slackly run.

A crimson dawn leapt from the eastward. They picked up the pilot and by noon *Leviathan* was anchored amongst the waiting fleet. Giorgios Botsaris sighed as he rang off main engines. Another voyage completed; he could catch up on sleep after last night's vigil … he hoped he could be left in peace for a few hours. The Hull Cleaning gang could be left to the chief officer. They were already on the scene, preparing for their second scrub. *Leviathan* needed it, because the Pencra job had been only a skim to remove the worst of the weed.

She would moor alongside this afternoon and begin loading at six. A tanker's life never stopped; though the dipping was now automatically operated, cleaning and pumping continued throughout the twenty-four hours. The Hull Cleaning people would be starting on her bottom tomorrow, leaving her slab sides until she was loaded in three days' time and down to her marks. He would like to meet the chap who ran the outfit — a large, blond man whom Botsaris had seen on the deck of the diving boat at Pencra.

The master never felt totally at ease when *Leviathan* carried a passenger. He had problems enough keeping his mixed nationalities of officers up to the mark. He was a martinet, he recognized that, but no one must underrate him because of his rotundity which was caused by this tanker life. He did not relish exercise, as did some of his officers who spent most of their time in the pool — and Botsaris walked slowly across his bridge to survey the anchorage.

The tankers were anchored in lines, like ships at a naval review: VLCCs, the 100,000 tonners and even one or two vintage ships, with their bridges forward. An extraordinary sight they were, as they waited their turn for the black fluid for which the industrial world craved. The 'Sea Island' terminal here at Kharg Island had been especially provided for the ULCCs who, because of their draughts, could load only at two other terminals in the Persian Gulf: Halul off Qatar, and at Muscat.

The pilot had clambered over the side and was waiting to be lowered by the mechanical ladder to the launch waiting out of sight ninety feet below *Leviathan*'s deck. Jonathan Krivine was being given a lift ashore with the pilots, but the boat trip took three hours to Bandar Rig, the nearest port on the Iran coast, where he was to meet the Lloyd's agent. Giorgios Botsaris hoped that there would be no hitch at this last moment; as soon as the scrubbing and the insurance were completed, he would be thankful to be under way again and into the cool of the Indian Ocean. The loading should be finished on Thursday, 21 April, but the sides' cleaning could not be completed before Friday, the twenty-second, at the earliest. *Leviathan* should be under way by Saturday, 23 April. He watched the diminutive launch swerving from under the hull, her wake churning white as she surged to full power. Jonathan was gazing upwards from her sternsheets, and waving. Giorgios raised his hand, then walked slowly back towards his wheelhouse; the radio officer was waiting for him, a telex in his hand.

The agent's office was air-conditioned and functional. Tom McGovern, a bustling, efficient Scot, had been expecting Jonathan and, after shutting the door, he came straight to the point. The four-bladed fan revolved lazily in the ceiling, stirring the air, while they downed their whiskies.

'There's no hurry, Krivine. Our launch will put you back on board when we've finished.' Jonathan liked this direct, no-nonsense agent.

'It's a relief to be able to talk,' he said. 'Any news from London, Mr McGovern?'

'Tom, please. Nothing special. They'll cover her on your say-so, if you're satisfied. We can get straight through from here.'

'*Leviathan*'s efficient enough. Botsaris is a good master. Runs his ship well.'

'London has asked about the safety precautions, particularly her reactor emergency shut-down procedure.'

'It's all automatic, Tom, and the chief can always scram the reactors if he has to. He has only to push the button.'

The Scot's sandy eyebrows were half-moons. 'It's all a mystery to me. Collision is what we're afraid of.'

'When she is scrammed the rods are withdrawn and the kettle only simmers — instead of boiling,' Jonathan explained. 'She can be fully scrammed automatically, on all four reactors. The chief seems a good hand and the Americans have built in all the safety measures. I reckon she's all right from what I've seen and from the little I know.'

McGovern remained silent. He glanced towards the door, got up and checked that it was firmly shut. He returned to his chair, then faced Jonathan squarely. 'And suppose the ship is hijacked?' he asked quietly. 'Could terrorists blow her up if they forced their way into the engine-room?'

Jonathan did not answer; he had been so obsessed with all the technical details which he had been checking during the voyage that the fantasia of high-sea piracy had never entered his head.

'It's a long chance, surely, Tom? Even if hijackers boarded her at sea, instead of from a terminal, what the hell could they do with her?'

'If they can hijack aircraft, why not tankers? And the bigger the better ... *Leviathan*'s a valuable bit of ship.'

Jonathan drew in his breath as he watched the imperturbable Scot tapping a cigarette on the packet he had slipped from his pocket. A fantastic idea, but not an impossibility, in these brutal days of political blackmail. Tom McGovern was leaning across the table.

'I met a chap yesterday who's out here on specialist work with the Saudis. His job — and they pay him well — is to pick up any intelligence he can from the Israelis. He's well in with the Arabs too, advising them on purely military matters. A friend of mine for years — came out with me after Korea. He's tipped me off; says it's genuine.'

'The ULCCs?'

'Could be — that's why I asked whether Planeka's ships are taking any steps to prevent hijacking. There ought to be some sort of policy as to what action to take if they're attacked.'

'Does London know about the threat? We can't hold up *Leviathan*'s cover on a say-so.' Jonathan was beginning to feel irritated; he had put in a lot of time and trouble during this tedious trip. McGovern's smile was condescending:

'I'm not suggesting anything of the sort. We should cover her now, if you're satisfied. But only subject to PSI taking steps to prevent a take-over — realistic measures, agreed by London. You should insist on this, Jonathan.'

McGovern sat back, watching the smoke curling towards the extractors. 'That's my recommendation. I'm prepared to put it in writing.'

Jonathan glanced through the windows. The brownish-green water was flecked with white horses as the evening breeze sprang up from off the land. Out there, invisible beyond the shimmering horizon, the costliest ship in the world lay at anchor, ripe for the picking. 'I'll get through to my syndicate now, if I may,' he said. 'I'd like to talk to Lethbridge.'

'Certainly. At least we've got a day or two in hand. *Leviathan* can't sail until those Hull Cleaning people have finished the job. They've flown out their gear for this job, but I understand they're duplicating their service out here by forming a Gulf company. An efficient lot. It's run by a fellow with the same name as yours.'

Jonathan felt the jolt of mixed pleasure and surprise.

'David Krivine? He's my twin brother.' He grinned as McGovern walked across to the radio in the corner. Three minutes later, David's voice was crackling through the loudspeaker.

'Meet you tomorrow in Tom's office,' he said. 'I can't get there until after dusk. Stay ashore for the night and we can get out here again together, early tomorrow morning. Your ship's too damn big, Jonathan…'

The radio went dead. Jonathan was grinning stupidly — not everyone could understand the affection that one twin felt for the other. Out here in the Gulf, personal problems seemed remote and utterly unreal.

'Well, Captain,' Jonathan said, sipping the whisky which Giorgios Botsaris had poured him when he had finally returned on board the next day. 'Your ship's fully covered for all risks. You can sail when you like.'

The Greek master pursed his lips and slowly wagged his head. 'The owner will like that. He doesn't like me hanging around too long. These ships cost money.'

'But there's one thing we insist on, Captain…' Jonathan said, watching the master assimilating the conditions upon which Lloyd's were insisting. 'Lloyd's want to agree anti-piracy measures. They want me to fly back to work things out with your owner.' He smiled as he contemplated the Greek's leathery face. 'Once they're agreed, Lloyd's want me to sail with you once more to help you as much as I can with the drill. If we both know what action to take should you be molested by hijackers, Lloyd's can assess the risk better. They'll reconsider the rate next year, if PSI will co-operate.'

'I think we can put up with you for another trip, Jonathan,' Giorgios chuckled. 'You'll join us again at Pencra?'

Jonathan nodded. 'About the twenty-fifth of May.' He pulled out his diary. 'Depends on the anti-fouling, doesn't it?'

The master had risen from his chair. He strolled to his desk and picked up a telex sheet.

'Nothing's certain with Planeka,' he said ruefully. 'But this beats the lot, Jonathan. And I thought that Kartar Browne's god was money...,' and Botsaris sucked in his breath through his gold-capped teeth. 'He's always put profits before the good of the ship or her crew. Now I don't understand him,' and Botsaris wagged his head again. 'Listen to this...,' and he began reading aloud the two-page telex.

The message was from PSI's head office, an amplifying directive to her master, explaining that the ship was to continue with her original programme and to proceed to Pencra for anti-fouling — in spite of the enquiry from the States that she should discharge her full cargo in America, *at a considerably better price than at Pencra.*

'Kartar Browne's never acted like this before,' Botsaris said incredulously. 'He's turned away good money. He could have postponed the anti-fouling.'

'Perhaps he thinks it cheaper to make use of Hull Cleaning Services? Once you've been slotted into the Pencra schedule, is it difficult to reserve a berth again once you've cancelled it?'

'Not impossible.' Botsaris shook his head again. 'Doesn't make sense.'

'The locals kicked up such a row before they accepted a nuclear; Browne's worried about the politics,' Jonathan insisted.

He was surprised at Botsaris's reaction. The master was striding to-and-fro across his stateroom, muttering to himself. He stopped in his tracks, his cheeks flushed: 'What's the point of my sweating my guts out, Krivine, trying to save every hour of unproductivity in order to cut down these ULCC losses, if, the moment the ship can pick up a good contract, the opportunity is turned down?' He swore a Greek oath and thumped his fist into the open palm of his other hand. 'Does that make sense to you?' He strutted across the carpet again and flung himself into his chair. 'Forget it ... forget it, Jonathan. I'm fed up with this waiting. I'm exaggerating, but it's enough ... how do you English say? It gets on my tits.'

They laughed, then Jonathan swallowed his whisky. He had much to do and he had to fly back to London tomorrow.

CHAPTER 15

The heat was shimmering across the Kuwait runway, like the aura before one of David's migraines. He waved for the last time towards the World Cargo freighter lumbering down the runway. Inside were Alf and his skeleton crew, jammed amongst the final load of gear they were flying home. David slumped at one of the tables and ordered a beer. He extracted the crumpled programme from his pocket and slowly drew a line through today's items; it was twelve days since *Leviathan* sailed and he hoped he would not have to live through days like those again:

Sat. 23 April: *Leviathan* sails from Kharg to Pencra.

Sat. 23 April: Clean crawlers and gear.

Sun. 24 April: Weekend off for crews.

Mon. 25 April: Start moving crawlers and gear from Kharg Island to Kuwait. Tom has arranged crews' air tickets.

Fri. 29 April: All gear ashore at Kuwait. Transport firm takes over, for onward packaging to UK.

Sat. 30 April: Run ashore at Kuwait for crews.

Sun. 1 May: " " " " " "

Mon. 2 May: Skeleton crew remains. Alf Kelway i/c.

Remainder of crews fly home to UK — 1 week's leave.

Alf starts supervising loading crawlers and gear into World Cargo freighters.

Tues. 3 May: Last loading day.

Thurs. 5 May: Alf and skeleton party fly home with last of gear.

(*Leviathan* due Pencra 19 May.)

David paid for his beer, glanced at the smudge vanishing into the ochre sky above the desert. Alf should be at Le Bourget, Paris, by this evening, hijackers permitting — then on to Helston tomorrow, the old Fleet Air Arm airfield which they had opened up for civil use. HCS was up to date on schedule so far:

Fri. 6 May: Crawlers and gear at Helston.

Sat. 7 May: Skeleton crew 1 week's leave. (Alf to take leave after *Leviathan* sails again from Pencra.)

Mon. 9 May: Crews return from leave. Move gear from Helston to Falmouth.

Tues. 10 May: Start servicing crawlers, working with *Pelican*.

Mon. 16 May: All crews back. Prepare for skim and one-coat anti-fouling of *Leviathan* (ETA 19/5).

Thurs. 19 May: *Leviathan* berths Pencra. (I fly Concorde Bahrein to Heathrow ETA 11.15.)

Fri. 20 May: *Pelican* alongside; prepare crawlers for Monday.

Sat. 21 May: Weekend.

Sun. 22 May: "

Mon. 23 May: Start skimming port side of *Leviathan* and finish?

David tucked the worn sheet back in his pocket: he would need a crystal ball to plan further than that … even if there was no strike, something must fall down somewhere.

Tom was a good agent: not only had he seen to all the bookings, but he had eased the path for this next week's difficult negotiations, a tough assignment with meetings morning and afternoon for the whole of the next fortnight. David would be starting tomorrow, meeting the top brass for setting up Hull Cleaning Services (Kuwait). If he ran into no snags, he could make the Concorde flight on Thursday 19 May.

Knud had said he would meet him at Terminal Three, Heathrow, when the monster bird touched down at 11.15, London time.

The Arab waiter shuffled across, bored, a buttoned-up face, giving nothing away...

'Whisky, please — no ice.'

The man was in his fifties, his face lined by hardship. An incredible transformation in one man's lifetime: from tent to air-conditioned flat in less than ten years. Kuwait would become one of the most modern cities in the world, though sited in an unbearable climate. Not so long ago these Arabs were kicked around by the rest of humanity. Now, an Arabian businessman bought one of the proudest ships in the world as if he was shelling peanuts — and London sale rooms resounded to auctioneers' hammer blows: Mayfair properties, Rembrandts and Turners — all were being knocked down to these *burnoused* brethren. Even the most devastatingly powerful nations on earth dared not set foot on this wretched sand to grab the precious black stuff lying beneath...

It was good to sit back for a moment. He could relax on Sunday, but there was nothing lonelier than a modern hotel if you were by yourself. He had disliked saying goodbye to Jonathan, after picking up with him again. David had pierced the veneer which his twin brother had acquired, and they were back again to the old days when, as kids, they had been inseparable.

Jonathan was certainly doing well for himself, acting as Lloyd's special envoy. He had flown back to the UK on the day before *Leviathan* had sailed, and he had hoped to spend the weekend of 23–24 April with his Margaret — she was a good sort, though incapable of concealing her disapproval of David's way of life. But one day she might discover what it felt like, if her world disintegrated about her. Johnny had hinted that he might not yet have finished with *Leviathan*. He was returning to London and would be at Lloyd's on Monday, 25 April.

Today was Thursday, 5 May ... fourteen days before his Concorde flight home on Thursday, 19 May; he would have to sleep in Bahrein the night before, to catch his flight at 09.45. The fare was considerably more expensive than the Tristars, but they were fully booked; Knud had insisted on David being back that Thursday, because he had to see him about the monitoring device before travelling to Aberdeen.

David's estimate to Sally had not been far out — six weeks. The mails had been regular to Kharg, but then her letters had ceased. He had not heard from her since he had come over to Kuwait. He had rung Tom; he would forward anything on to David's hotel...

The whisky was doing him good, unwinding him — now all he wanted was his woman. He was worried about her; he would ring her tonight, when she was sure to be at home.

'Fasten your seat belts, please. We are now beginning our approach to Heathrow.'

The smooth voice of the hostess dragged him from his dreams of those golden moments which Sal and he had shared in the early days. They seemed long in the past — and he winked at the hostess who was smiling at him contemplatively.

'No smoking, please...'

The Concorde was a fine aircraft — after taking off at 09.45 from Bahrein, she had banged through the sound barrier and was now, less than four and a half hours later, dropping her snout for the run-in to Heathrow; 11.15 touchdown, she would be bang on time. He might as well have travelled in a silver bullet: he had seen nothing. For an extra 150 pounds he had gained one and a half hours on the Tristar... How quickly could he be shot of Carlsen? He could catch the Penzance express, if the Dane did not keep him too long... And how would Sally be looking? Tired and grey, as when he had left her, heavily pregnant? She had retained the glint in her black eyes when she had seen him off, but he was worried about her. Her phone calls had been strained, and she had not been at home when he had rung her these past two nights. He would travel down to Trefusis tonight, if he had to rent a car and drive...

The Dane was waiting for him by the Customs' barrier. He stood head and shoulders above the crowd, a scarlet carnation in the buttonhole of his brown tweed suit. He was puffing a cigar and flapping a *Financial Times* in the air.

'Glad to see you, Dave. Just got time to brief you before my Aberdeen flight. Everything's great, just great,' and he thrust David towards the crowded lounge. 'Here, this'll do...,' and he subsided onto one of the settees. 'How'd you like Concorde?'

Knud Carlsen was certainly trying to erase the memories of the *Sumba* episode, while David brought his new boss up to date on developments in the Gulf. 'I've got them interested in forming the Kuwait company,' he added. 'I've found storage and a site for the crawlers.'

'Fine, Dave, fine.' Carlsen slapped David across the back. 'We'll order the next eight for the Gulf immediately. You'll see to it? Carrick again?'

'I'll get down to it, after the *Leviathan* job's finished. We're starting on Monday, if she's up to her ETA.'

Carlsen stubbed out the stump of his cigar, lit up another. Between the ritual puffs, he summarized events of the past weeks:

'Company's doing fine … capital's okay … only a fortnight before I've finished with Planeka … saw that bastard Browne … hairline in anti-fouling … couldn't care less … profits only interest … ordering three more ULCCs…'

'Two coats of anti-fouling?' David asked. 'The paint company guarantees it — almost neat arsenic.'

Carlsen nodded: 'We'll know more about its efficiency after this next voyage. The monitors'll give us what we need to know.' He puffed again, watching the smoke curling upwards. 'My American bright boy has sent over three more monitors, different to the others,' he added, 'to be fixed between D15 and 16, and on either side of the Mark Is. He insists on concentrating on this area; thinks the cause may be connected with contorted eddies from the bulbous bow. We can forget G25 and 26. I told the guy we'd be happy to co-operate. Okay, Dave?'

'A few more devices won't be any bother. When can you let me have them?'

'As soon as they arrive from the States. He's despatched them TWA. You'll have to fix them at the last moment. I'll bring them down myself.'

'With the others?'

'Yeah … at the same time, I'll let you know what sensitivities to set. Any idea, yet, what day you'll be finished, what day she'll sail?'

'We could be wrapped up by Tuesday, the thirty-first,' David said. 'She'll finish discharging that afternoon.'

'Okay. I'll be down that afternoon, but let me know if there are any changes of plan. You'll secure the plastic pods before, or after, you paint?'

'I'll paint first.'

Carlsen smiled apologetically: 'Of course, Dave. But you won't have to fix the monitors for G25 and 26 now — the Yank says they're redundant.'

'Good. I've enough on for the last day. Have you arranged with the ship's officers to stop the condensers and circulator inlets, while I fix the after monitors?'

'Yes. They're quite happy — and, by the way,' Carlsen added, 'Alf Kelway phoned; he'll be meeting your train, so look out for him, he told me to let you know. Okay?'

David glanced at Carlsen. Why not Sally? But he seemed to be hiding nothing.

The Dane had risen to his feet: 'See you next week. Give me a ring if you have any problems.' Then impulsively, he encircled David with his disengaged arm. 'Swell to be partners, isn't it, Dave? Just swell,' and he beamed with avuncular contentment. 'My flight's from the other terminal. I'll ring when I get back,' and he bustled off, soon to be lost in the crowd.

David hurried to a kiosk and started feeding in the ten-pence pieces. He could see in his mind the phone by the entrance to the cottage, just behind the door. If the sun was out, the shadows of the nodding fuchsias would be dappling the whitewashed wall. Sally would be trying not to hurry across the stone-flag of the uneven floor...

He let the phone ring for two minutes by his watch. He thoughtfully replaced the instrument, picked up his bags and wended his way down to the British Airways bus which was waiting outside.

CHAPTER 16

From Exeter St Davids onwards, David had been unable to contain his unease. The sun was already low as the express snaked along the foot of the Dawlish cliffs, red and wet from the plunging seas that were breaking across the sea defences. More than two hours yet before Truro — why was Alf meeting him and not Sal? Plymouth, Saltash and Brunel's bridge, the long climb up to the Moors, then Bodmin — he had already collected his bags in the corridor — and the train was thundering down the run-in to Truro. He hurried into the corridor, to be first at the door...

Alf's figure flashed past the window, his drawn face peering intently ... and then David was bundling out, the door crashing back on its hinges.

Alf was coming towards him, a smile frozen on his face. David had never seen him in other than his working clothes, but tonight he was in brown slacks, the collar of his shirt out-turned upon his sports jacket. He had shaved and his face shone with the well-being and inner contentment that seemed to glow from men like him. The crofters and the fishermen of Ross seemed to share the same serenity, reflected a similar inner peace through the tanned, clear skin of their faces.

'Hullo, sir.' Alf had always refused to follow the modern practice of using Christian names. ('I like to know where I stand,' he would tell the younger ones.)

'Hi, Alf,' David said. 'Nice of you to meet me.' He paused, then asked: '— and where's Mrs Grant?' He fixed Kelway with his eye. 'Why's Mrs Grant not here, Alf?' He plopped his bags on the platform. He pinioned Kelway's arms to his side. 'Where is Mrs Grant?' he asked softly.

Alf was doing his best; he had come here to help. 'She's in hospital, sir.' Then he added hurriedly: 'She's okay, sir. My Belle's been with her.'

'Your wife?' He let go Kelway's arms. 'How long's she been there? Is it the baby?'

'Yes, sir, she's in the maternity hospital. They've been very good to her — took her in last week — Sunday, I think it was. Belle went with Mrs Grant, sir, so she's all right.' Alf had picked up David's bags and was leading him to the red Mini parked outside the station. 'I'll take you to the hospital now, sir.'

'Thanks all the same, Alf,' David said. 'I'd rather go on my own.'

Kelway nodded, then let in the clutch. 'I'll drop you off at the cottage.'

David watched Kelway, his dependable 'number one', whose strong face was etched against the headlights of a crossing car. Alf had been a first-class Outside ERA; and he was as excellent a right-hand man in HCS; David wished only that he could pay him more. 'How's the work going, Alf?' he asked quietly.

'Everyone's back from leave, sir. *Leviathan* berthed this evening. *Pelican*'s moving out tomorrow.'

'Got all the stores? Anti-fouling arrived okay?'

'Everything's arrived. Don't worry, sir. All set for Monday...' So the journey passed, the two men discussing the details of next week's vital work on *Leviathan*. David told him of his progress in setting up Hull Cleaning Services in Kuwait.

'It's going well, Alf. We'll get all the work we need, if we make a good job of *Leviathan*.' Then he elaborated upon the extra monitoring services which Carlsen wished fitted. 'We'll be years ahead of our competitors.'

'The pods have arrived, sir. I've got 'em all on board *Pelican*.'

'What are they like?'

'Transparent plastic, pear-drop shaped; strong magnetic strips are built into the padding of the flush base — they're easy to fix.'

'Good — they've changed the plans a bit. I'll put you in the picture tomorrow,' and David collected together his things, as the Mini's headlights swept through the crooked lanes of Trefusis village. Seconds later the white-washed cottage was bathed in light.

'Give Mrs Grant our best wishes, sir. Belle will be up to see her tomorrow.' The Mini growled and disappeared into the night.

Without Sal, Fuchsia Cottage was as lonely as the depths of the ocean. She'd left a note on the kitchen table dated last Sunday: 'Come straight up to the maternity hospital, darling. They're taking me in, just in case your young gentleman is on the way. Don't worry about the office; everything is up to date. Sal.'

That was all; in the kitchen everything was in its place, a tea-towel spread across the washing-up bowl. He nipped upstairs to their room; their bed was ready and turned down; close to her side was the bassinet they had chosen — they had settled for white, a compromise to blue and pink. They had become very superstitious during the long wait — but this was her last chance, the doctor had said — and, as David extracted from his bag the roll of flowered silk he had bought for her in Bahrein, he remembered the discussions they had shared, late into the early hours sometimes, as to the morality of deliberately creating a child in their unorthodox marital status.

'Out of wedlock,' she had said, but neither of them had sniggered.

'But you are my husband, if not legally,' she had told him so often. 'That's not important to *me*. It's how you are in God's eyes that matters. He won't condemn our child.'

'The world will,' David had said quietly. 'Even in these days, society can be cruel.'

She had pulled his face round so that she could search his eyes while she emphasized her words. He could see her green eyes, even now, two fires flickering with an intensity he had never seen in any other person. 'Does it matter what others think?' she had murmured across the pillow that early morning. 'I want your child, my darling, before it's too late ... you've always said you believe in God. He's brought us together, you said. He'll bless our child.'

'Are you sure, Sal, we don't manipulate our God to suit our wishes?' They had forgotten their dialectics when her arms encircled him ... and that had been eight months ago. Was their God punishing them for taking his name in vain? Damn his puritan upbringing and the tap-roots of his father's Jewish religion — and he bustled from the cottage to the tumble-down garage.

The sister, who had been so considerate last autumn, was making up her report when David tapped on her office door. She looked up, this woman in her forties, her face lined by the acceptance of suffering. She looked worn out, her blue and white uniform soiled by the day's interminable crises. A cloud flickered across the gentle face, as her brown eyes searched his.

'Mr Krivine?' she asked. 'I've been waiting for you.' She slipped her pen into her pocket, climbed to her feet and came towards him, her rubber-soled shoes silent on the polished floor. The wards were ancient and stank of disinfectant, but a happy atmosphere hovered about the place…

'How is she, Sister?'

She touched his sleeve. 'As well as can be expected, Mr Krivine. You mustn't be alarmed when you see her.' She smiled up at him: 'All quite straightforward, you know: the saline drips and the blood. She's quite safe now.'

David halted in the corridor.

'What's happened, Sister?'

'She picked up an infection — slight septicaemia.' The sister paused, then looked away, apparently lost for words. 'I'll leave you together, Mr Krivine,' she said quietly. 'She's quite able to talk now. She wished to be the first to see you. I promised her, you see…,' and the severe face was looking up at him, serious as she weighed him up, judging him. She pushed open the door of Sally's room: 'Someone to see you, Mrs Grant.'

He hesitated in the doorway; this change in Sally was too shattering, in spite of the sister's warning.

'Sal…'

He moved to her bed, clasped the small hand lying upon the sheet; her veins were blue rivulets in the translucent grey flesh.

'I'm glad you're back,' she said softly. Her tired eyes were barely open, dark pinpoints in their sunken sockets. She was wearing her best nightdress for him, but it was stained where they had tried to find the vein. A battery of bottles was slung from the pedestal by her bed. A tangle of plastic tubes descended to her forearms, to her nostrils. Dabs of sticky plaster criss-crossed her skin, holding the life-saving impedimenta in place.

'Not very beautiful,' she whispered, 'for my returning husband.' She managed a smile and he had to turn away.

He took her hand: 'You're doing fine, my Sal,' he said, and then he saw how slight she was beneath the linen. If he blew upon her, she would vanish on the air...

'Our child?' he whispered. 'Girl or boy?'

Her fingers were clenching his. She was trying to speak, but her lower lip was trembling. 'Oh, David,' she began. She could not go on and suddenly she turned her head upon the pillow.

'He lived three days,' she whispered. 'Until last night.'

She stretched her other hand to him. He did not know how long he stayed, stroking her hand. But when the sister came, she was asleep, drained of all emotion and strength.

'You can stay here the night, Mr Krivine,' the woman whispered as she led him from the room. 'I'll put a chair in her room for you.'

CHAPTER 17

The first twist of the knife, Jonathan felt, was that today, Saturday, 28 May, must be one of the most glorious days this year. If the sky had been leaden with rain and there had been an east wind cutting across the headland, this ordeal would have been easier to bear, for all of them.

I am the resurrection and the life, saith the Lord: he that believeth in me, though he were dead, yet shall he live: and whosoever liveth and believeth in me shall never die...

The eternal words were growing louder, as the cortege approached up the path. Jonathan turned in his pew to gaze blindly at the rectangle of light which was the entrance to the chapel. The scent of gorse wafted from the golden heads nodding about the doorway, while the song of the birds outside formed a continuous accompaniment to the priest's words; the portal darkened; the cortege halted, then moved inexorably up the aisle.

...We brought nothing into this world, and it is certain we can carry nothing out. The Lord gave and the Lord taketh away; blessed be the Name of the Lord...

A black marionette at the head, another at the foot of the minute coffin, the priest leading ... the rigid figures of Sally and David staring before them, refusing to glance at the oaken box being lowered before the small altar whereon stood the wooden cross; Belle Kelway trying to stifle her weeping, Alf with his arm about her.

It was the unnecessary cruelty of it all that seared Jonathan's thoughts at this moment. What purpose could this little tragedy serve? How difficult to believe that this was Divine planning.

To him, this was callous cruelty, for David had intimated that the specialist had forbidden Sally to attempt another child. Sally, David had said, had acted on her presentiment and had arranged for the hospital priest — the same man of God who was standing before them now — to christen little Andrew on his third day of existence. When the virus had ended his short life, Sally had, for eighteen hours, retreated inside herself with despair. According to Belle, who had never left her side, Sally had then suddenly rallied; she had never betrayed a trace of self-pity and had been unbelievably stoical. Perhaps it was her faith, a faith stronger than his own... Jonathan was finding it impossible, at this moment, staring at the diminutive oaken box, to accept that God was merciful...

St Paul's words seemed so terrible, so incongruous, almost barbarous, on this shining May morning in this peaceful churchyard...

Be not deceived: evil communications corrupt good manners. Awake to righteousness and sin not; for some have not the knowledge of God.

How did David reconcile that one...? Sally had asked that the service should be as cheerful as possible — she looked so fragile, in her flowered dress and scarf, standing by the man she loved. According to Alf, David had been thrown completely by the tragedy; it was Sally who had been the rock, she who had sustained him throughout the long week during which he had to persevere with cleaning the big tanker.

Perhaps the ordeals of the past had rendered David more emotional than Jonathan ... his brother's large shoulders were heaving momentarily, and then Sally's and David's hands were entwining. David was squaring his shoulders, lifting his shaggy blond head to stare defiantly towards the cross.

What, dear God, is he thinking now? His twin brother could react so tempestuously, a slave to his emotions as he had always been … and those frightening words of his up on the cliff-top weeks ago, swept back into Jonathan's mind… 'I'll kill him, Johnny. I'll throttle him with these hands of mine, if her child is taken from her. Kartar Browne will have murdered it, just as I'll kill him…' These were terrible memories to recall in this place.

…Behold I show you a mystery: we shall not all sleep, but we shall all be changed, in a moment, in the twinkling of an eye, at the last trump … so when this corruptible shall have put on incorruption how could this flicker of life that had been Andrew be called corruptible?… *Death is swallowed up in victory. O death where is thy sting? O Grave…*

Jonathan longed to stop his ears from the awful, wondrous words. He tried not to listen, to concentrate instead on the posy of primroses at the coffin head, on the flagging bluebells at the foot which Belle had picked … the priest was gently leading David from his pew — this was Jonathan's cue … and he slipped into the aisle, waiting at the foot of the coffin for David to lift the head.

He almost allowed the box to slip from his hands, it was so light. The two mourners in their dark suits stood aside, became vague shadows; and then he and David, the coffin borne between them, were blinking in the sunlight as they slowly followed the chanting priest.

Man that is born of woman hath but a short time to live… In the midst of life we are in death…

It had been the callousness of the world and the inhumanity of bureaucracy which had nearly driven David berserk during the past week, Alf had confided to Jonathan. Saturday morning had been the only possible moment for David to be present at the funeral — but the gravediggers needed double time for working on Saturday morning — and the office of the Registrar of Births, Marriages and Deaths had been shut at five minutes past five when David had arrived to register the death. 'No burial without a certificate; the office opens at nine-thirty tomorrow...' It had been too much for David's sensitivity and his patience.

He and David must be careful now. The hovering spectres glided to his side, adroitly transferred the weight of the coffin into the bights of the ropes...

The mounds of flaking shale at the graveside; the mica in the soil glinting in the sun; the whiff of damp earth; the depth of the hole — it all seemed obscene on this glorious morning. Jonathan stood back, making room for Sally and David to approach the graveside.

...We therefore commit his body to the ground [the rattle of the Cornish soil upon the coffin lid was utterly final] ... earth to earth, ashes to ashes, dust to dust; in sure and certain hope of the Resurrection...

Jonathan wrenched away his eyes, gazed across the fields to the distant sea; the bay shimmered, silver and blotched by the shadows from the scurrying clouds sweeping up from the Scillies ... a scurry of lapwings tumbled overhead, flapping and pee-witting in the wind. The air was rich with the scent from the resin of the pines bending and soughing in the gust.

Lord, have mercy upon us,
Christ have mercy upon us,
Lord, have mercy upon us.

And then the beautiful, ancient words of the prayer which their earthly father had taught them from the earliest days which Jonathan could remember — he repeated them mechanically, his memory recalling vividly the blond child with the broken wrist, the David of seven years, trying not to blub...

...and forgive us our trespasses, as we forgive them that trespass against us. And lead us not into temptation; but deliver us from evil.

No innovation could replace the dignity of these immemorial words…

So this little soul had quit our selfish world to return to his Maker? Did he really believe this, *could* he believe it, considering the life he led, his maelstrom existence, chasing his tail merely to keep on the same spot? A man needed such a moment of truth to confront the blurring of his fundamental beliefs which modern life engendered. Politics, the battle of existence: such things bore little relevance to that hole gaping in the soil at his feet.

Silently he moved away, leaving Sally and David alone by the graveside. He had not the courage to face his twin brother; he yearned to fling his arms about David, weep with him as his forefathers would have done, unleash the grief that was aching within — but he never could, for were they not both from the stiff-upper-lip brigade? Instead, he must slip away… David would understand that his underwriter brother must get back to Margaret, for the ritual weekend. If he escaped at once, he could just catch the train; then there would be no need to lie to David about his rejoining *Leviathan* on Tuesday morning. David had said that he could not be finished with his final underwater inspection before the evening of Tuesday, 31 May.

'You're David's twin, I believe?'

The priest was removing his vestments, folding up his stole. He had appeared from behind the gates to the cemetery where he had been talking with two men — probably the diggers waiting to fill in the grave.

'Yes, I'm his brother,' Jonathan said. He respected this greying man, with the sad, resigned eyes, who had conducted the burial service with such simple dignity. He must have performed this melancholy duty thousands of times during his ministry. David had said that the priest had been just the man he needed — authoritative, but kind. *We take these men of God for granted, most of us*, thought Jonathan. *We seek them only when our primordial instincts yearn for solace* ... and Jonathan was finding it hard to meet those level, compassionate eyes.

'How much, sir, should I...?' and he nodded towards the men hovering by the gate.

'I'll see to that, Mr Krivine,' the priest said. 'I was wondering how close you are to your brother?' and he strolled a few paces towards the turf beneath the pines.

'We see each other infrequently,' Jonathan said. 'Not as often as we should like. We were very close when we were kids.'

'He's told me a bit about himself,' the priest said. 'He's had a difficult life...'

Jonathan sensed that he was being invited to divulge confidences — if only he had time, but he'd miss the train, the only rail connection to make his return to Sheppey worthwhile.

'David's been through it recently, sir,' Jonathan said guardedly. 'I'm worried about him too, particularly, after this...' and he inclined his head towards the cemetery. 'David's head is ruled by his emotions.'

The priest was extending his hand.

'You mustn't miss your train, Mr Krivine. If you need me, please get in touch.' He added spontaneously: 'David is in need of help, Mr Krivine. I fear for him, for what he may do. He cannot accept this...' and he, too, glanced towards the chapel beneath the trees. He shook his head. 'He's taken it badly. He's very bitter, Mr Krivine. He finds it difficult to accept the ways of the Lord.'

'Don't we all?' Jonathan added softly. 'Difficult to understand sometimes.' He paused, then said: 'You see, sir, this was their last chance for a child.'

The priest stood motionless, his white surplice flapping in the breeze.

'I didn't know,' he said softly. 'I never knew,' and he turned towards the sea. 'Goodbye, Mr Krivine.'

A lark soared suddenly. It broke into song, trilling high above them. Jonathan peered upwards, trying to trace the source of this paean to creation. He searched the blue sky until his eyes watered, but he could not see the little bird.

CHAPTER 18

Through his driving mirror David watched, first the gates of the cemetery and then the clump of pines vanishing from view. Sally sat by him, her hand on his thigh, staring in silence through the windscreen as he drove back to the cottage. Alf's Mini was waiting outside.

'I asked him to be here, Sal,' David said. 'I'm going straight down to the ship.'

'I'll get you something.'

He helped her into the cottage. Belle was there, an apron about her as she worked over the stove. A white tablecloth was spread and there was a smell of stew. She came and took Sally from him.

'There, my dear. We'll all be better for something to eat.'

'I'm going down to the ship, Sal.' He kissed her and went outside. Alf put him into the Mini and drove off down the winding lane.

'The work'll do you good, sir. They'll be waiting for us.'

David Krivine extracted the revised schedule from his pocket and forced his mind to absorb the details of his formidable programme. The work had been crippling all the week, for every man in his team — and thank God for it, at this time. He scrawled a pencil line through the items up till 28 May: what came next?

Sat. 28 May: (A.M. Funeral Andrew) 2nd coat stbd side — ABC.

P.M. *Oswald* secures pods after painting patches — (M.D. and A. Kelway).

Lev. starts cargo discharge P.M.

Sun. 29 May: 1 coat port flat bottom — ABC.

Oswald touches up rudders and 'A' bracket fairings.

Lev. cargo discharge. Tank trimming.

Mon. 30 May: 1 coat stbd flat bottom.

Oswald completes bulb.

Lev. cargo discharge.

Tues. 31 May: A.M. Delivery of 4 Mk I Monitors (G25 and 26 have been cancelled).

Crews clean and service gear.

Fit monitors: Y3 & Y4; D15 & D16 (*Oswald* — M.D. and Kelway).

P.M. *Oswald* (spare crew) hand-paint shafts and propellers. (Alert ship's staff to brake shafts.)

P.M. *Lev.* completes ballasting and prepares for sea.

19.30: Delivery of Mk II monitors.

20.00: Final underwater inspection and fitting of 5 Mk II monitors (Kelway to take charge of spare). Alert ship's staff to shut cofferdam inlets alternately.

Pelican crew weekend leave. Tugs move *Pelican* to South Mole.

22.00 (approx.): *Leviathan* sails.

'*Oswald*'s all ready. The inflatable's standing by, sir. I'll drive for you while you fit the pods.' They left the Mini on the jetty and scrambled down the steps to the Zodiac.

David crouched abaft the spray hood, as the rubber boat bounced across the bay to *Pelican* who was secured on *Leviathan*'s port quarter.

'So you've got the crews started, Alf. Thanks.'

'Didn't want to waste time. The lads are in the swing and we should have both sides skimmed by tomorrow night.' He throttled back on the Mercury, as Arthur Tregent, *Pelican*'s skipper, leaned over the gunwale to take the painter.

'Welcome back, Dave. The pods and *Oswald* are all ready for you.'

David nodded, walked aft to shift in the crew-room. He was lucky in the team he had gathered. They swore, they drank, they scrapped in pubs, but they had bloody great hearts. He slipped into his skin suit and joined Alf by the divers' caboose forward. *Oswald* was waiting for him, swooshing in the swell, the pods visible in the retaining basket.

'All set...'

He never noticed the water, it was so warm. *Oswald* was behaving impeccably, as always; Alf took her down, following the vertical white lines he had slapped on *Leviathan*'s sides, sides which, by tomorrow, Sunday, would be gleaming with fresh paint: she had finished pumping days ago.

The skim with the new wire scrubbers had been more successful than he had hoped. Her sides were smooth and clean — this Auto-Burnishing-Copper (ABC) paint was excellent stuff. The more turbulent the area on the bottom, the greater the amount of biocidal solution released — and the more the paint reacted, the smoother the underwater surface became. Because the anti-fouling medium and the biocidal material in the ABC were released under chemical control, the lifetime of the product's effectiveness could be calculated by measuring the thickness of the paint. The ship's bottom would remain free of growth whilst a layer of paint remained; and so a planned cleaning programme could be laid on with Hull Cleaning Services. If the monitors could provide further statistics to improve ABC, Hull Cleaning Services would be leading the field.

The dappled light of the surface was receding when Alf switched on the lights. David signalled for *Oswald* to be halted where the first white rectangle glowed — the patch scraped off at Y4. He extracted the first plastic pod from the basket and, holding it well clear, gradually approached the hull until he felt the magnetic pull. When precisely over the marks, he allowed the pear-drop pod to clang into position.

'Okay, Alf,' he burbled through his intercom. 'Across to Y3.'

A smooth bottom was an important factor in the efficient operation of big ships. Weed killed speed and even a one-knot decrease could lose an operator £250,000 in one year on his ship if he included dry-docking in his downtime costings. By applying ABC anti-fouling, the hull became smoother with use and time. So, if Planeka maintained a regular anti-fouling programme, the hulls of its fleet could be guaranteed operationally efficient for at least four years, provided the ships were initially properly cleaned and prepared.

'She's okay, sir?'

David shook his muddled head; he must not allow his weariness to affect his concentration on the job in hand. Alf had manoeuvred *Oswald* spot-on above the next patch: clang! — and pod Y3 was neatly in place.

'Down to the next line, Alf — D15 and 16.'

Oswald swung aft, weaving sedately beneath Alf's experienced hands.

Why should he, David, worry about whether Planeka's fleet saved millions a year by using HCS's techniques and services? He felt an insensate anger welling inside him; it was a cruel irony that he should be making his money from the ill-gained wealth of that bastard, Kartar Browne — the doctors had told Sal that the loss of her child was caused mainly by stress and overwork. How negligible would have been the worry and work without Browne's double-dealing and extortion... If Kartar Browne had played straight, little Andrew could have been with them now ... a red mist was swirling before his eyes and then he wondered whether he might be suffering from a touch of the bends. He checked his gauges — okay. He had better watch his step and not allow this obsessional hatred to get the better of him...

'Here we are, sir.' Alf's imperturbability was a balm when things were tricky; there was the first patch, D15 — *Oswald* was crawling towards the painted Glo-line rectangle — and then, clang! another pod was in place.

'Follow the line across, Alf. D16 next...'

So it was athwartships across the ship, to the port side. The scrubbers had certainly done a good job, but they had not entirely scraped off the hairline running transversely here — the crack in the old paint which he had reported. The Dane would be down on Tuesday, 31 May, to hand over the monitors. David would be interested to know what Browne's reaction to the hairline had been.

'That's it, sir... Surface?'

'Take her up, Alf. Thanks.'

The sun was breaking through the surface. They would grab a breather before their next dip to see how the crews were getting on with the second coat on the starboard side. He would be glad to be starting on the 'flats' tomorrow.

It was difficult to realize that, less than eighteen hours ago, he had been standing with Sally at the graveside of their son. The church clock was chiming three; within the hour first light would be stealing through the honeysuckle invading their bedroom window. So this was Sunday, 29 May, the beginning of another week. No week could ever again be as terrible...

He stroked the soft hair of her head lying in the hollow of his shoulder. He could see the outline of Sal's pinched face, asleep at last, exhausted from the emotional tempest through which she had passed. What could she have been thinking when finally merciful sleep overcame her? Did she suffer the same bitterness, a similar hate which he felt for Browne and all his works, a loathing which David was now almost enjoying? Looking down at her, he wished he could have borne this week with her fortitude...

He never dreamed that he could ever experience the emotion, the quality of tenderness ... yet, with this fragile little body tucked into the crook of his arm, no better description suited the feelings which the tough, worldly David Krivine was feeling at this moment. 'My Sal...' He whispered her name, the very name which gave him the strength for which he yearned, the power to shove this destructive malice behind him ... and he slowly turned his head towards the window.

He must finish the *Leviathan* job, then escape for a day with her to regain his composure. They could run up to Boscastle, perhaps to Hartland ... gradually she might regain her health; together they could pick up again the life they had left behind. It was curious how he did not want her now. That would come, he supposed, as she returned to life. He had never before been like this, putting his woman before his own desires.

Sunday morning already... Sally had said she wanted to go to that good man's church. If Alf could start the crews on time, David could leave them to finish painting the port 'flat', once *Oswald* had given them the line. Then he could return after lunch with Alf to finish the difficult rudder area. *Leviathan* had long been well out of the water, more than eighty feet of her side showing. She would be trimming tanks and ballasting today and tomorrow, but that would not affect the crews.

It was strange how casually Carlsen had taken the hairline evidence, but then he, too, hated Kartar Browne's guts. Curious, also, why Knud had virtually bribed David to keep his mouth shut — 'A bonus,' he had said. 'We want to keep this to ourselves, Dave. We'll be years ahead of our competitors.' Such yarns were nothing new in the diving world...

The meeting with the ship's officers had gone well. He had liked the Greek captain who had, with his chief engineer, been co-operative; they had shut each cofferdam inlet alternately, so that the divers could work safely on them. The engineers would repeat the temporary shutdown on Tuesday at 20.00, when he would make his final inspection before she sailed. Tomorrow, Monday, would see the completion of the 'flats' and *Oswald* would have completed the bulb.

Would Tuesday never come? He felt poised on the razor's edge — and not only because of the importance of this contract. He sensed an unease he could not explain ... was he losing this woman he loved above life itself?

He turned drowsily towards her, gently stroking her hair while he watched her breasts rising and falling. How would she accept the fact that, unless the doctors changed their minds, not until middle-age would they again be able to make love in utter abandon? Would that spoil something precious, or would she take the risk — and could he allow her to jeopardize her health for their mutual pleasure? Of one thing he was certain: never again would she be the same Sal as before her tragic pregnancy ... and his eyelids were drooping again.

He had only two more days' work on *Leviathan*. There was something not right about the whole contract, something he could not pinpoint. Carlsen's organization worked efficiently enough; he was sending the monitors down by car, complete with technician, to advise David how the gadgets should be fitted into the pods. Ten o'clock, Tuesday morning, down at the jetty ... roll on bloody Tuesday, roll on...

CHAPTER 19

It was curious how her mental state had changed — and she wearily discarded her apron and went outside to sit in the porch under the fuchsia. It was good here, feeling the sunlight beating off the white-washed mud wall — but now, after the agony of the last week, she yearned for the first time to be able to call herself Mrs David Krivine. No matter if they could never have a child, no matter ... she had her David. He should be able to survive these last few hours on the *Leviathan* contract, but he was very near breaking-point. In addition to his personal tragedy, he had borne the whole burden of administration, as well as taking his share of the manual work. He had been diving now for the past ten days. She would cherish him during these next two days on the north coast — there was no lovelier corner of England. She smiled to herself, as nostalgic memories flooded through her. Perhaps they could recapture those golden days...?

Unusual that he should be so unpunctual — late lunch he had said, because the Mark I monitors were not being delivered until ten o'clock this Tuesday morning. He had then to fit them with Alf, so he could not possibly be here until one-thirty; but it was half-past four now. She had long ago stopped trying to keep the roast chicken hot, a bird she had bought from the farm next door. They had been so good to her during these past few months: Juliet had never asked questions, merely been there to help when she was needed. A comfortable person — understanding, perhaps because she had no children ... the Ford was grinding up the lane. She jumped up and scurried into the kitchen.

She hovered over him whilst he hurried through the meal. He gulped down the beer, remained silent while devouring the cockerel and roast potatoes. He peered up at her, patted the seat alongside him. 'I love eating out here in the sun,' he said. 'Thanks, Sal. Wish I didn't have to hurry, but I've got a lot to do before I pick up the final load at nine-thirty.'

'Can't Alf supervise it for you, David?'

'I want to be sure the job's properly finished, before the ship's staff take off the shaft brakes. Anti-fouling those huge propellers and the shafts ain't easy, gal...' He pulled her roughly to him, smacked a kiss on her cheek. 'Five hours and it'll be all over. We'll make an early start tomorrow. I've got a room at Hoops.'

He looked at her and, for the first time in months, she recognized that gleam in his eye. She was still worried about him, she realized; the more intense the pressures, the more remote he was becoming. She was sure he was concealing something from her.

'Don't worry about me, Sal. A good sleep and I'll be on form.' She pushed his hand away. It was too early yet...

'Why are you so late?'

He recounted his frustrating day: the monitors had arrived an hour late.

'So we lost an hour. Carlsen sent them down in a Merc, but the driver lost his way. The technical boy went over the drill with me at least three times — Peter Honak. He's a nice guy — nutty as a fruit cake, but thorough. They're neat contraptions, beautifully made. They slipped into the pods as easily as kiss your arse.'

She chuckled while she poured out the last of the beer. 'Why have you got to go down again, David? I thought you'd finished.'

'My final inspection. I'll fix the Mark IIs at the same time.'

'What's the difference between the two monitors?'

'The Mark IIs are an improvement on the Is: they work on a different principle.'

'I'm not so dumb as I look. David...'

'The Mark Is are designed to register the marine growth in the less turbulent areas and they have to be hand-set. They are switched off at the moment. Carlsen's boys are giving me the key tonight to set the sensitivity, last thing. The Mark IIs are self-setting, which is why they're larger. They're just in from America and have the advantage of being able to register the turbulent areas. They're dual-purpose, able to fit inside the pods, as well as attaching themselves magnetically to the cofferdams.'

'What time are they delivering the second batch of monitors?' She worried when he was late; she was concerned by his lack of concentration, though she knew he was as competent as any diver in the business. 'You're tired, David.'

'"Seven-thirty this evening on the jetty," Knud said. I hope they'll be punctual this time.' He glanced across at her. She had shivered involuntarily, as the sunlight dulled. 'I'll fetch your shawl,' he said. 'There's a fog in the offing.'

'What time's twilight end, sir?' Alf asked, stamping his feet on the greasy jetty. 'This lot 'ud be late for their own funeral.'

'In two and three quarter hours — 22.23. It'll be dark earlier tonight.'

David felt the clamminess eating slowly through him. Visibility had shut down; every twenty seconds the doleful blast from the foghorn on St Anthony Head was reverberating across the harbour. 'The chief said he'd keep the cofferdams safe until we had finished.' A miserable evening, this, for finishing off their first big job; visibility was less than a cable, but Alf knew his way blindfold to Pencra and he had fitted the serviced outboard to the Zodiac.

'Here they are, sir.' The rattle of a car's diesel grew louder through the mist. 'Same Mercedes — quarter of an hour late.'

The big saloon bumped along the wooden slats, slid to a halt, its wipers flicking half-moons across the windscreen. The driver remained at the wheel, keeping his engine running. Three men jumped out, and two of them scurried to the boot. The third, a large character in a dark coat, approached David.

'David Krivine? Mr Carlsen asked me to give you this.'

'Yes...' There was a thickness in the man's voice which David could not place — certainly not English. 'Thanks.'

'Sign here, pliss.'

Scribbling his initials, David asked: 'Isn't Peter Honak with you? I was expecting him to be handing over the Mark IIs.'

'Flying back to the States. He said he'd instructed you thoroughly and you'd know what to do. He asked me to give you the setting key for the Mark Is... That's what you've signed for,' and the man laughed shortly. 'Here it is. He's typed the setting for you. It's in the envelope.'

'Thanks.' David turned towards Alf: 'How many Mark IIs?'

'Six, sir.'

'One's a spare,' the big man added. 'In case you lose one underwater. Mr Carlsen asked that you phone him when the job's finished. He's sorry he couldn't get down himself.' This bunch were in as great a hurry as Alf and he.

'Okay, Krivine? We've got to get back to London tonight.'

'Thanks,' David said. 'Mind how you go.'

The doors slumped shut. Alf was lugging the cartons down the steps. The driver touched the horn in farewell and the Mercedes vanished into the fog.

'Didn't waste much time, once they were here,' David said as he unhitched the painter. 'Got the lot, Alf?'

'Yes, six in all. They're heavier than the last lot.'

'Stow the spare in *Pelican*'s caboose, Alf. Shove off.'

The outboard coughed into life and then the Zodiac was creeping past the piles as it widened the distance from the jetty. Alf kept her parallel, then slowly opened the throttle. David settled himself down, abaft the spray cover.

'Can see bugger all,' Alf called. 'Watch out for Black Rock, sir. I'll take care of Pendennis.'

Ears were as useful as eyes in this stuff. Alf was reducing the revs, his head cocked, listening. The slap-slap of the wavelets on the rubber hull ... then he heard a coughing of diesels, off to port.

'Port beam,' he shouted. 'Powerboat of sorts.'

Alf raised his hand. His red pom-pom and his eyebrows were glistening with droplets — and then they spotted the blur of Pendennis. David could hear the waves swooshing on the rocks of the foreshore. Alf was extracting the pocket compass and slowly opening the throttle again. The steady frapping of the boat's flat bottom was the only sound above the Mercury. Then David heard it again: the distant diesels of a fast powerboat. He slanted his arm across to port:

'Bloody fool,' he yelled. 'Ought to know better, in this lot.'

The bay was stiff with holiday sailors at this time of the year. The clatter of fast-running diesels passed up their port side, disappeared ahead. David extracted the envelope from his pocket, checked that he had the vital setting-key. Alf would be alongside *Pelican* in a few minutes, and the less they had to do on arrival, the quicker the job would be finished. It would soon be dark: the fog was shutting down more densely every minute. Arthur Tregent had been on duty non-stop for the past fortnight so David had sent him ashore for the night; Alf and he could complete this job themselves. He would take Alf down with him to fit the three Mark IIs: one between the two Mark Is already secured at D15 and 16, the other two Mark IIs on either side. At the same time, he would set the sensitivity switches on all the Mark Is; and he felt again in the pocket of his anorak — the key was safe there.

He could manage the last of the Mark IIs on his own. He would not take long to slip one into each cofferdam, as they were self-fixing. Alf could watch things up top and begin shutting up shop, always a tedious business…

Opening the envelope, David extracted a buff-coloured sheet which fluttered between his fingers, as the Zodiac bounced towards the whistle buoy off the northern mole. The instructions were typed and were signed by Knud.

"'David,'" he read. "'All Mark Is are to be set to with the special key. I hope to get down to see you on Thursday.'"

It was 20.25 and almost dark as the massive blur of *Leviathan* loomed out of the fog. The Zodiac bumped alongside *Pelican*'s battered side. *Oswald* was hooked on, ready for hoisting out.

'Get the generators going, while I find a lanyard for the setting key,' David ordered as he nipped on board to secure the inflatable. 'I shan't need you for the after part, Alf, but it'll be quicker if you drive for me during the inspection. We'll start on the port quarter; I'll fix the settings when we reach the fore section.'

'What are the settings, sir?' Alf had always been a prudent diver.

'Plus nine,' David shouted over his shoulder. 'All Mark Is — Plus nine.'

CHAPTER 20

The fog was swirling in thick gobs around *Pelican*'s deckhouse when they finally surfaced. They could just see, inset halfway up *Leviathan*'s side, the flush bollards for the tugs' warps when she was in ballast. Alf had lit up his post-dive fag, one of his few habits. David waited with him for a few minutes, to regain his breathing and collect his thoughts. *Pelican*'s floodlights threw an eerie pool of light upon the slippery decks but, apart from the whistle buoy, the only sound in the night was the splashing from one of the discharges on *Leviathan*'s quarter.

'I've just spoken to the chief on the intercom,' David said. 'I've told him I'll report to you as soon as I'm clear of the cofferdams.'

'Okay. I'll contact him at once.'

'It will soon be finished, thank God. Only the last two Mark IIs to site. What have you done with the spare, Alf?'

'It's in the caboose, sir. Hope you won't need it,' and he grinned. He had always considered himself a better diver than his boss. He was trained — and he had not done a year's clearance-diving for nothing, after leaving submarines.

'Start clearing up when you like,' David said. 'I should be surfacing within the half-hour.'

'Take it easy, sir. Belle's not expecting me home till late.'

'All set?'

'All set, sir.'

So the last stage in this mammoth operation had at last been reached — and David sighed with relief as he took down *Oswald* for the last time. His spirits lifted suddenly; he felt unnaturally elated, happy-go-lucky, like someone with the bends. The crawler was working superbly well, but perhaps it was because they had become used to *Oswald*'s idiosyncrasies by now. Carefully checking the areas around *Leviathan*'s stern, he took the crawler slowly towards the cofferdam inlets. The lights plainly illuminated the red bottom, remarkably smooth now that the work was finished: Hull Cleaning Services had certainly done a good job for Kartar Browne — the bastard...

David was watching the inlet current — he would not enjoy being sucked in — but the chief engineer was reliable and could be trusted — there it was ... the dark hole, two yards in diameter, the cofferdam where both the condenser and reactor circulator inlets were sited. A neat arrangement this, each with its own hull valve and independent cross-connection.

He worked carefully — no mistakes at this stage. He lifted the penultimate monitor from the basket, gripped it, then slipped the device against the for'ard side of the cofferdam. Shoving it inside as far as he could reach, he turned the convex side towards the for'ard edge of the cofferdam — then let it go. He heard it clang home; tried to shift it — but it was fixed rigidly. If it shifted, it would be sucked in only more tightly against the grilles. It would be interesting to know what results it produced, particularly on the reactor readings.

He climbed back on to *Oswald* and piloted her across to the other side. Same procedure again, but with even more care — then, as the last of the monitors snapped home, he swam back to the controls of his crawler. He took her clear, piloting her for'ard along the bottom until he was thirty yards clear of the cofferdam. He paused there to contact Alf on the intercom.

'A-okay,' he reported. 'Job's finished. The chief can open up his inlets.'

The garbled voice acknowledged his report. It was all over ... up to the surface, only a few fathoms above him. In seconds he glimpsed the luminous popple between the two hulls — and then he was up.

'Right, I've got you, sir.'

So it was all over. He pushed back his mask and sloshed for'ard along the wooden deck.

'Thanks, Alf. That's it. Home to Belle…'

He did not at once notice the tension in Alf's face. 'What's wrong, Alf?' David asked. 'Is the chief worried?'

'No, Sir. Come into the caboose — something to show you.'

Alf, who was already in his shore clothes, led the way. David followed him, flippers sloshing, and stopped in the doorway. Alf was facing him, the opened case of the spare Mark II monitor in his hands.

'Couldn't resist having a look, sir,' he said quietly. 'Wasn't difficult to open — five screws.'

'But where are the guts, the electronics?' David asked. 'And what's that?'

'The only guts are a timing device, sir. And this…'

They turned when the heard a pattering on the deck for'ard of the caboose.

'Hang on a moment, sir,' Alf said softly. 'This is explosive — modern stuff. Enough to blow a hole the size of a double-decker bus. Look — here are the detonators. Same as we had at *Vernon*.' His eyes were boring into David's, when suddenly he glanced behind David's shoulder. '*Watch out, sir!*'

Alf sprang forwards, toppling him off balance. David scrambled round. Four skin divers, their wetsuits gleaming in the floodlighting, were advancing silently towards them. Each held a knife in his hand.

'*Scarper, sir!*' Alf yelled, hurling himself at the nearest of their attackers. 'For God's sake — quick — over the side.'

Alf had no chance, as he flung himself at the first man, knocking him sideways. The man slipped, and David staggered forwards in his flippers. Alf grabbed the knife which had clattered to the deck. Then he launched himself at the other three attackers.

It was all over in seconds. A knife flashed, stabbed, thrust, then stabbed again. Alf rolled to the deck, blood spurting from his mouth and seeping through his shirt. Two of the murderers reached down and flung the body over the gunwales, as the third man loped towards David.

David took the only way out, slumping backwards, the gunwale hard against the small of his back. As he rolled over the side, he glimpsed the grin on the face of the advancing murderer, saw the white teeth gleaming inside the mask. As David hit the water, he slipped on his facemask, ducking below the surface to adjust his breathing mixture. Don't panic — for God's sake *think* ... and then he saw the gloom of *Pelican*'s hull above him. He kicked twice with his legs, then stayed there, frozen motionless, regaining his breathing.

He heard the splashes as they hit the water, right aft. They were assuming he must be downstream — they were splashing about, floundering around her transom, five yards away. He could see their bubbles frothing on the surface as they vented. He might reach the Zodiac, for'ard, if he was quick...

Glued to *Pelican*'s bottom, he edged his way for'ard until he saw the outline of the rubber hull. The burbling of the killers' water noises were less distinct now, so he carefully broke surface alongside the Zodiac, between its curved rubber side and *Pelican*'s planking. He slipped back his facemask and rolled himself into the inflatable.

He slipped backwards against the Mercury, heard a yell from the darkness at *Pelican*'s stern. He swung off on the starter, his heart hammering against his ribs. His fingers were trembling as he rove the lanyard again and then he swung once more — another splutter — and then he recognized from aft the thick voice of the man he had met on the jetty. He could see their heads in the water — they were almost on top of him — and then the Mercury coughed, spluttered, and roared into life. *Not too savagely with the twist-throttle ... gently ...* with his free hand, he grabbed his diving knife.

The first attacker was emerging into the light, his mask gleaming black, when he lunged with his knife at the rubber hull. David opened up the throttle, nearly capsizing her as she jerked taut. He slashed at the painter, slashed again, and then she was slithering along *Pelican*'s sides. She was disappearing crazily into the darkness, the Mercury running at full belt, when he heard the hissing above the motor and her bouncing on the sea. He prodded the rubber, felt the wall subsiding as the air escaped. He would never make Falmouth. He turned to port, putting the sound of the whistle-buoy astern. He kept the throttle wide open, the boat pounding more and more until she was almost waterlogged. He'd kill himself if he continued. He throttled back — and suddenly it was very dark.

The chuckling of the water from the Mercury's cooling system was the only sound. The Zodiac was a deflated, limp sausage in Falmouth Bay. Those killers would not let him escape. Modern powerboats had radar; they'd be listening. He cut his engine. It coughed, died.

How long, God, how long since this frightful turn of events began?

These thugs were hired killers, paid to dispose of the only two individuals who could possibly know of the fixing of what were, in reality, lethal explosive charges.

In a flash, he could see it all, the ghastly mess: Browne and Carlsen had been in league all along, using him as their stool-pigeon to do their dirty work ... sink the ship, a total loss in deep water. But they had failed: he, David Krivine, was very much alive...

The silence was unnerving after the racket of the Mercury ... only the slap of wavelets again — but then he heard the sound of breakers, seas washing up on a beach, off to his left... It was only a mile and a half from the buoy at Pencra to Nare Head, at the entrance to Helford river. How far had he travelled in that crazy race in his dying boat? Several minutes at least, and at full speed he might have covered a mile. Whatever happened he must keep that sound of the swell on the beach to his left — he must not miss the Head and be taken up river. Thank God, he still had his suit and flippers. He listened again for the surf, for the waves breaking on the rocks, welling back and forth in the swell. Then he heard another sound, diesels, fast-running diesel engines...

He was shaking, whether from shock or fright, he could not care less, but his limbs were trembling. *Krivine, you're windy, bloody scared stiff. They're after you, those killers — and they'll get you, boy, if you don't think fast. They'd have ship-to-shore radio ...* then the realization of what might happen to Sally jerked him back to cool thinking.

Sink the Zodiac, without trace — it'll sink like a lead balloon if I leave the engine attached. Swim ashore. Find the nearest phone. Get Sal to fetch me — that'll get her away from the cottage. He slipped his knife from its scabbard, slashed repeatedly at the inflated half-section of the Zodiac. It gurgled beneath him and he kicked himself clear. He began swimming towards the sound of breaking surf.

CHAPTER 21

The white ribbon of surf was slightly to his left, a half-moon of regular curling waves on an open beach. A few yards to his right were the breakers, walloping lazily across the tops of the rocks drying at high water. The beach, which sloped steeply from the sea, could only be the coastline in front of the fishing hamlet of Porthallow. A high, black cliff reared up to the left. Below it, a wave was thumping across a pinnacle of rock beneath the headland which could only be Porthkerris Point. He swam steadily until he felt the back-tow, then touched bottom.

He emerged from the water, then saw the two fishing boats drawn up above high-water mark. Behind them, tucked under the cliff to the right of the lane running down to the cove, was the pub, its white walls barely visible through the mist which lay across the beach like a shroud. Porthallow ... and he felt the undertow again as the swell flung him upon the beach. He scrambled to his feet and staggered up the slope before collapsing onto the grey shale.

He did not know how long he lay there, fighting for breath after his long swim — minutes, seconds? He realized only that he was alive; that Alf was dead, his butchered corpse swilling out on the ebb into the Channel ... and then, clearly above the soft scrabbling of the shingle, he heard the deep drumming of *Leviathan*'s hooter — one long blast of at least five seconds. There followed the double toots from her tugs, manoeuvring in the fog. They would have already shifted *Pelican*, without her crew as he had arranged, so that the ULCC need only slip her bridle and steam straight out, around the head of the northern mole and to sea...

He had lost all sense of time, all power of thought. God, oh God, was this nightmare reality? Was he living through this? And then his brain began to function again, forced by stark actuality to face facts.

His watch showed just after 23.00. His escape to the shore must have taken a good twenty minutes — so the Mark II 'monitors' must have been positioned at about 22.30. The Mark Is must have been set at plus nine, half an hour before that. *Zero hour 22.00.* Each second that slipped by was now reducing the time when, presumably, those Mark I settings would run out — at *07.00 this morning.*

Alf had been certain the stuff in the Mark II devices was explosive... 'This is explosive — modern stuff. Enough to blow a hole the size of a double-decker bus. Look — here are the detonators...' He could hear Kelway's voice now — he had been certain, sure as ever Alf Kelway could be ... and the proof of Alf's suspicions lay in those stealthy killers who had slipped on board from the fog. A powerboat was messing about in the darkness out there now — he could hear its fast-running diesels moving slowly up to the northward ... and the sinister presence of his remorseless hunters stirred David to action ... *one hour wasted already.* He must seek help, get Sally, go to the police, warn and stop the ship. He wrenched off his flippers and floundered up the beach, the shale painful under his soles...

He must phone Sally to come down and fetch him. She'd corroborate his story with the police. But speed, *speed...* He staggered to the pub and battered upon the door. A curtain was thrown back and a voice was shouting from inside. The bolts were withdrawn and then he was blinded, blinking in the bright light.

'Good God, man!' The landlord, a man in his thirties, stood there, his mouth open. 'You gave me a turn...' He held out his hands to catch the man from the darkness from collapsing on to the stone flags. 'Hey, Janet! Come here and give us a hand.'

The woman, still in her curlers, bustled him into the kitchen and began fussing over him.

'Your phone ... can I use your telephone?'

The man and the woman were glancing curiously at each other. David raised his voice: 'It's bloody urgent,' he shouted. 'A man's been murdered and they're after me ... and that's not the least of it.'

'Here, in the bar...'

They switched on the light, the sour stench of beer hoisting him back to reality. He listened for a full minute to the ringing of Sally's phone. He slammed down the instrument, swept back the hair from his forehead. 'No reply ... my God, they've taken Sal...'

'Here, mate, knock this back...'

The rum reached his guts, and slowly his head ceased swimming ... that launch would be in direct R/T touch with its masters ashore. They would have pinpointed Fuchsia Cottage. Carlsen *must* be behind this, with Kartar Browne... And to ensure that David did not squeal, they would hold Sally hostage until after the big bang...

Belle, he'd ring her, she'd come down for him ... but she would be in no state to vouch for him — he could not suddenly confront her with the brutal murder of her husband. The news would have to be broken to her as gently as possible... Arthur Tregent, reliable, sturdy old Arty, skipper of *Pelican*, who had a house in Gweek...

They looked up the number for him, the woman's finger trembling as she turned the pages... T... R... E... David stood over them, itching to help... 'Tregent A., Quarry View, Mawgan 17,' she read.

The phone rang for an eternity before Arthur was on the line. 'David, you all right? Right. Porthallow...'

The woman wrapped David in a blanket. The man lent him a shift of old clothes. When Arty arrived, they slung David's diving gear into the boot of the old Vauxhall.

'Thanks,' he called to the doorway as Tregent drove off, 'I'll be in touch. If anyone other than the police contacts you, you know nothing — *nothing*.' As the car began its climb out of the combe, the glow behind the bar window flicked out.

'Straight to Falmouth, Arthur,' David blurted out. 'To police headquarters. I'll put you in the picture on the way.' The Vauxhall was crawling up the lane towards Tregarne, the beams of its headlights transforming the space ahead of them into thick soup.

'For Christ's sake, Arty, get a move on,' David snapped. 'Every second's vital, can't you understand?'

He glanced at his wristwatch: 23.40 — one hour and forty minutes had already been irretrievably lost.

The yawning constable behind the counter strolled to the rear office. The tousled duty sergeant emerged, buttoning up his collar:

'Name, sir?...' and he proceeded to search for the report book. 'Address?... All right, sir, all right. Take it calmly, sir. Now what's your story?' He fixed David with a suspicious stare. 'Slowly, sir. We must have the facts.'

By the time the duty sergeant had roused out the duty inspector, David had at last begun to shake things up. 'Can't you see, Inspector, this is desperately urgent? A bloody good ship is out there, steaming south into the Channel. She's a nuclear tanker and she can explode at any second in relatively shallow water. *There're thirty-eight men on board...*'

The grey-haired man was scratching his head. 'Just a minute, Mr Krivine. I'll have a word with the assistant chief.'

Five minutes passed before he was back.

'He's coming down. We should like further proof of your story, Mr Krivine. After all, you've nothing to show us, except that you're a bit uptight.' He smiled apologetically.

David glanced up at the old clock on the wall. He lost his temper, banged on the counter with his fist: 'Send someone to Mrs Grant's cottage in Trefusis. I'm sure she's been abducted.'

'Calm down, sir. Sergeant, fix Mr Krivine a cuppa...'

It was twenty-eight minutes past midnight when the assistant chief constable strode into the station. Hands in his raincoat pockets, he tried to weigh up the situation.

'My name's Balk,' he said. 'Charles Balk, assistant chief. We've heard about your work on the tankers, Mr Krivine. Come into my office and tell me exactly what's happened. You say a man's been murdered and a ship's about to blow up if we don't act fast?' He glanced at the harassed David. 'Okay — and you think Mrs Grant's been taken as hostage by this mob to keep you quiet until the devices beneath the ship explode? If that's the case, we had better send a car to Trefusis, Inspector. Take a look at the cottage, while I have a word with Mr Krivine. And Inspector...'

'Sir?'

'Issue side arms. If you find evidence, report to me at once. Then I can act. Full precautions, just in case. *If* Mr Krivine's incredible story is bona fide, these villains are killers.' He motioned to the chairs: 'Now, Mr Krivine, start at the beginning…'

Glancing occasionally at Arthur, David launched into an account of the past twenty-four hours: 'It wasn't until Kelway showed me the explosive in the spare Mark II monitor, that I had the faintest clue that we had just fixed explosives to the ship's bottom.'

'No suspicions at all, Mr Krivine? Didn't Carlsen give anything away?'

David shook his head.

'Think back … for Pete's sake, man, can't you recall anything?'

David stiffened in his chair. 'Yes, there was my report on the hairline crack. I was surprised Carlsen didn't take it more seriously.'

'He had parted brass rags with Browne — hated his guts, you told me,' Balk prompted.

'Yes — but I can see it now. He's got me to place the extra Mark IIs along the hairline. So there really was a hull weakness … and with the main ballast flooded for'ard, she'll break in half like a wafer biscuit.' He took the sheet of paper which Balk was pushing across to him. 'Here, sir … and here.' He sketched in the positions of the magnetic, explosive charges.

'And two big ones in the condenser and reactor circulator inlets, you say?' Balk queried. 'If they explode, they'll blast two holes into the largest compartment in the ship.'

'Her engine-room's colossal, sir. No watertight subdivision. If that's flooded, she'll sink like a ton of lead.'

'And there's no setting on the Mark IIs?'

'No — but the smaller charges are switched to plus nine.'

Balk was stroking his nose with his forefinger.

'We can presume that the units are in hours. There's no report from sea yet of any big bang or sinking — the coastguard always let us know of any incident. So the Mark Is should go off at seven am, if you had set the switches at ten. Right?'

David nodded and glanced up at the clock: 'That's why I'm het up, sir; time's slipping by. The Mark IIs could explode before...'

The assistant chief sprang to his feet. He strode to the Admiralty Chart, showing the Western portion of the Channel, which hung on the wall.

'Here,' he said. 'This is the prescribed routeing for the ULCCs using Pencra. Help me track *Leviathan*'s course...'

David jumped up, traced the red route on its south-easterly course.

'Her speed's restricted until she reaches the 50° latitude,' Balk said. 'She then has to steer south, to cross the shipping lanes as nearly at right angles as possible.'

'She'll speed up,' David said, 'to get across as rapidly as possible.'

'Speed?'

'Eighteen knots, sir.' For the first time he smiled. 'We've just anti-fouled her, remember?'

Balk was pricking off her DR, taking her down to a red cross marked on the chart, west of the big E in the word 'Exercise' of the area used by submarines.

'That's where they are allowed to break off. If they're Gulf-bound, they usually steer 225° until they're south-west of Ushant.' He was pricking off the distance: 'She'll cross the 5° west longitude line at one o'clock — *plus three hours.*' Then he was marking off the distances run ... 'plus four hours,

02.00…'; 'plus five hours, 03.00'. At plus nine hours he was in a position 260° Isle of Ushant seventy-two miles.

'Add five miles for the tidal stream,' David added. 'It's springs.'

Balk curled a double red circle round the position. 'In about ninety-five fathoms,' he said. 'A steaming nuclear cauldron at the entrance to our Channel.' He scrawled, 'Plus Nine Hours' against the DR position. 'There,' he said, 'twenty-two miles south-west of Parson's Bank.' He looked up as the voice of the inspector came through the loudspeaker:

'Tango Lima One here, sir.'

The assistant chief pressed his transmit button: 'Balk.' David felt the blood pumping in his veins. 'Signs of a violent struggle, sir. The intruders have scrawled in lipstick on the kitchen table: "Krivine," the message reads, "KEEP OFF — if you want Mrs Grant back in one piece." Two capital letters K.C. after that, sir.'

'Yes?' Balk rapped. 'And what's the colour of the lipstick?'

'A sort of brick red — shiny.'

David nodded. 'Carlsen's played me all along, sir. He's been in with Kartar Browne the whole damn time.' He stared directly at Balk. 'They'll know I've come to you since they didn't manage to kill me.'

'That's where they've slipped up,' Balk said. 'I'm sorry, Mr Krivine, but we'll have to take a chance with Mrs Grant. There are thirty-eight men out there.' He looked across at David. '*Why? Why*, that's what I want to know? Why sink the biggest ship in the world, a tanker with nuclear reactors? Pollution politics, I suppose.'

'There's a determined lobby to prevent the building of these monsters,' David said. 'The world's too small a place now for the potential disasters which these ULCCs pose.' David turned to Tregent:

'*Why does Browne want to sink his own ship*, Arty?'

Balk butted in: 'Let's ask the man himself. And he's got to tell us when the Mark IIs will go up. We're wasting time. Where does he live? He's the owner, isn't he, Mr Krivine?'

'Yes — a big estate near Hertford, I believe.'

Balk was scribbling on his pad: 'Kartar Browne...' He was now fully in charge, attacking at last, his eye on the clock; its hands were touching the three-quarters past midnight.

'Get me the assistant chief, Hertford,' he snapped to the operator. 'Personal — yes. Get him out of bed.' He turned to David. 'Might as well try Carlsen — "Knud," you said? Beckenham?'

Minutes later Balk turned his back, as he spoke briskly into the mouthpiece of his phone:

'Charlie here. Yes, it's vital, Bill. Kartar Browne...' He etched in the chain of events. 'Yes, Ministry approval — outside territorial waters; flag of convenience. The navy, I guess. Who else can? The Minister?' Balk laughed shortly. 'We can do better ourselves...' He was scribbling again. 'Yes, yes... Triton Place; okay. Chopper?' He glanced up at the clock. 'Two-and-a-half hours, if he's at home?' Balk sucked in the air between his teeth, stroked his nose. 'Not before three at the earliest? Myself, Bill. Yes, Helston, repeat Helston. I can use the time to get things humming.' He chuckled. 'Thanks — not bloody likely. Without Browne we're... He'd better be at home, or else...,' and he rang off.

The instrument trilled immediately.

'No reply from Beckenham? Right.' He slammed down the phone.

'We'll have to concentrate on Browne,' he said, turning to David. 'We've no time to start searching for Carlsen.' He turned away, embarrassed: 'Mrs Grant will be all right, Mr Krivine. She's only of use to them if she's alive.' He put his hand kindly on David's shoulder. 'Come on,' he said. 'We've got a lot to organize in the next few hours. We've got to stop *Leviathan*, get her crew off and remove the charges. Bill will find Browne, if he's on his patch.' He glanced at David. 'Any ideas, Mr Krivine? You're a diver, I believe.' Then he added softly: 'We've got just over six hours, if our guesses are correct.'

In the silence, David could hear the clock ticking.

CHAPTER 22

Assistant Chief Constable Commander Charles Balk knew that this was the crisis of his career. A misjudgement or an omission now, and there could be the most catastrophic disaster, not only in human life, but in pollution from nuclear contamination of the whole South West. Then there was his own future... The chief was taking his time to answer his direct line: it was not very late.

'Yes, Charles?'

'I'd like authority to institute Full Emergency Procedure, sir...' It took time to sketch in the developments but, when he had finished, Balk added: 'I've gone to Channel Zero, sir.' The whole emergency network was on a common VHF frequency now — police, fire brigades, the military and the navy, RAF rescue helicopters, coastguard and lifeboats, and medical services.

'Right, Charles. Carry on till I get down. I'll ring London and the navy from here. Where are you setting up your Emergency Operations Centre?'

'Here, sir.'

'Couldn't be better. I'll get George Wood to ring you direct from Helston.'

'Thanks, sir. He'll do all he can.'

'A good exercise for his chopper boys.' The phone clicked.

Balk felt better — the chief constable was now sharing the weight. He was a good boss, leaving the details to his number one. Charles felt exhilarated by the emergency; it brought back vividly his few years in the FAA — he had used Helston twice in bad weather.

'The pilot's ready, sir.' The inspector was poking his head round the door.

'Good, Alec. Use 22.00 as zero time. Nine hours from the moment Krivine set the charges will be 07.00 — the Big Bang will be in Position *Zulu*.

'Right, sir. I've sent for Jim Brett: he's our best diver. When he gets in he can work with Krivine.'

'Get a move on. We've got to be at Helston by 03.00, in case the RAF chopper makes its ETA. Hertford gave 03.00 as the earliest time-forward.'

'Cars at two-thirty from here?'

'Yes. We'll stick together. Can't afford a balls-up.' Balk strode to the ante-room where Krivine was pacing:

'We're hoping the navy'll lift us out to *Leviathan*, Mr Krivine. Will you help us?'

The fair-haired giant turned abruptly, his face grey and drawn.

'Of course,' he said softly. 'I fixed the bloody things: I'll take 'em off. But I need more air, sir. I must have professional help if I'm to go down out there...,' and he nodded towards the Channel.

The rain was slatting across the window, now that the fog had precipitated. The wind was getting up.

'I'm giving you one of our most experienced men, Krivine. He'll be under your orders.'

'Thanks. I must have enough bottles: there are plenty in our store. And I need more gear: rope, buoys...'

'Take all you want. *Inspector*...,' and Balk called across to the other room. 'Car for Mr Krivine.' He glanced again at this professional diver: he wasn't capable of much more, by the look of him. 'You've got two hours; we leave for Helston at two-thirty.'

'Are you stopping the ship, sir?'

'Don't know yet. Depends on the navy.'

'She's still inside the fifty-fathom line,' Krivine said. 'We ought to let her reach deep water.'

'I agree. But if the navy can't take off her crew, she'll have to stop and abandon ship.'

'They may refuse to quit,' Krivine said. 'It's not a pleasant night for boating.'

The inspector stuck his head round the door:

'Brett's here, sir. The car's ready.' Krivine hurried out.

While Balk waited for his chief's call, he saw to his own affairs. He sent his driver home for his warm clothes; the inspector, Alec Pardoe, handed him a gun, organized details...

At 01.17, the chief was on the direct line:

'Hertford have picked up Browne,' the clipped voice said. 'The RAF should be taking off any minute.' Balk sighed with relief.

'The navy, sir?'

'Georgie Wood not through yet?'

'No...'

'I've talked to C-in-C, Plymouth. He's dispatching the emergency destroyer, but there's a snag: *Audacity*'s on a rescue job — yacht in collision with a trawler — twelve miles east of Start. She's being diverted immediately.' The chief sounded satisfied.

'Type 21, isn't she?' Balk said.

'Thirty knots, the staff reckon in these conditions. She can be in Position *Zulu* at 07.15.'

Balk glanced up at the wallchart, rubbed the side of his nose.

'A close thing,' he said. 'The charges, we reckon, will explode at 07.00.'

'We can't do any better, Charles. Perhaps that fellow Krivine is a few minutes out — plus nine was the setting?'

'Correct.' He could almost hear the chief's mental arithmetic...

'You're right. Seven o'clock.'

Channel Zero was crackling from the loudspeaker on the wall:

'I'll ring you back, sir.' Balk slowly replaced the phone as he listened:

'This is Fleet Air Arm, Helston: Captain Wood for Commander Balk...,' and then the commanding officer of the helicopter station was on the air:

'Morning, Charles. What can we do for you?'

'Can you put two divers and their gear, one passenger and myself on board a ship off Ushant?'

'When?'

'Any time from 03.15 onwards.' Balk glanced at the clock: '01.49 now — in an hour-and-a-half.'

'Position of the ship?'

'South-west of Parson's Bank.'

'Has she chopper landing facilities?'

'Sure to have — she's the most modern tanker yet.'

'Communications — can you get her to guard Channel 16?'

'I'd like to talk to her from your base, George. I've got problems.'

'Wait one...'

The only sound was the crackling of the radio on the wall. The inspector came into the office and stood fidgeting by the desk. Balk glanced up at him:

'It's a long way on a night like this, Alec — 270 miles, there and back. Add take-off and hovering time.'

'Brett's rung up.'

Helston came on the air: '...Captain Wood for Commander Balk... Charlie?'

'Balk here.'

'How much gear do your divers want to take with them?'

'About five hundred pounds, sir,' the inspector murmured.

'Five hundred pounds, George,' Balk repeated.

'Fine. There'll be a Sea King waiting for you. The station will be manned from 03.00. Full emergency procedure, then. I'm liaising with *Audacity*. See you...'

The wind was whistling across the Helston tarmac when the three police cars arrived at five minutes to three. They were waved through the gate and directed to the operations room.

'Sea King *Love Romeo*'s standing by,' Captain Wood said. 'The Royal Air Force have been through; your passenger should be landing at about 03.45, Charles.'

'Thanks. Can I get through to the ship while they load up the chopper?'

'Leave the loading to us... Perhaps Mr Krivine should also talk to the master? We've been trying to raise *Leviathan* through Land's End radio. She's not answering. The loudspeaker's switched through.'

Charles Balk tried to contain himself while they listened, first to the naval telegraphist, then Land's End operator, repeating and repeating *Leviathan*'s call sign ... finally the PAN... PAN... PAN was transmitted. The hands of the clock crept round its face until, at 03.42, the duty station commander put his head round the doorway:

'The RAF'S chopper's just coming in, sir.' Balk could hear the fluttering of a rotor somewhere overhead in the darkness. 'We'll transfer the passenger as soon as it lands,' Balk said. 'Can the Sea King take off at once, George?'

'If we have to. But I'd prefer to have *Leviathan*'s position first. *Audacity* hasn't got her on radar.'

The telegraphist's voice was cutting in: '*Leviathan* on the line, sir…'

'All yours, Charles…' Captain Wood handed the microphone across.

The foreign accent was tantalizingly close through the loudspeaker:

'This is *Leviathan* … this is *Leviathan* … do you read me?'

'This is Land's End radio. Emergency call for you, Captain … *over.*'

Balk came directly to the point:

'This is Emergency Operations Headquarters, Captain. We have evidence that explosive charges have been placed beneath your ship. They are timed to explode, probably at seven o'clock. That's in three and a quarter hours' time.'

There was a short silence and the faint sound of garbled discussion at the other end.

'What do you want me to do about it? D'you want me to stop?' the master asked curtly. 'The weather is not good.'

'Maintain your course and speed, please, and keep radio guard on Channel 16,' Balk said calmly. 'We're sending help. Can you stand by to take our helicopter? ETA 05.05, if you've been following routeing instructions. What's your exact position, please?'

'Okay, Chief… Wait please…'

Balk turned towards the naval captain who stood immobile, listening to the chat. Hands in his reefer pockets, white muffler around his neck, trousers tucked into half-wellingtons, George Wood would not commit his crews to unnecessary risk in bad weather. He must be given firm data…

'This is *Leviathan*… Land's End radio this is *Leviathan*…'

'Land's End radio… Go ahead, *Leviathan*…,' Balk replied.

'My position at 03.50: three-two-o — *Ushant* — forty-five miles.'

'Thank you, Captain. Your course and speed, please?'

'Two-two-five. Eighteen knots.'

'Your DR at 07.00?'

Balk could hear the background murmur of disenchantment, then the master was on the air again:

'Two-six-o — *Ushant* — seventy-four miles. I'll leave my floodlights on, though it will be daylight. Anything else?'

'Yes, Captain. A naval frigate is on her way to take off your crew. Stand by to abandon ship, please…'

Another long silence and then the astonished voice cut in again:

'In this weather? You want me to abandon ship?'

'Yes.'

'One moment, Chief. I have English man here. He can talk better.'

A cultured British accent came on the air:

'Jonathan Krivine, here. I'm a surveyor taking passage for this voyage. Can I help in all this?'

Balk turned to the diver standing behind him.

'Let me talk to him,' David Krivine said brusquely. 'He's my brother.'

CHAPTER 23

The master was not looking his best, Jonathan decided. Why was it that a sallow skin seemed to promote a beard more readily? Botsaris had been up since the PAN... PAN... PAN had come through; he was living off the drinks' machine at the side of the wheelhouse; he was sipping from the paper cup, and the steam from his coffee was condensing on the bridge window.

'We should see the chopper at any time now,' Jonathan said.

'I won't reduce speed unless they order me to,' Botsaris said. 'I can't take this seriously. There's some mistake.'

'You talked to Kartar Browne,' Jonathan prompted. 'He's in the helicopter.'

'I'll do what he tells me,' Botsaris said. 'He's the owner.'

Jonathan had given up remonstrating with the master. For the Greek, the affair was preposterous: first, the underwriters' insistence that their representative should take passage again to ensure that adequate anti-hijack measures could be put in force; and now, this drama. When Botsaris had recounted the tale to the mate, the officer had shrugged his shoulders, then stomped off in a huff. Who, in this filthy weather wanted to take to the lifeboats? But they had eased off on the gripes...

Jonathan moved out to the starboard wing, the collar of his coat turned up, staring to the nor'-nor'-eastward, as the wind buffeted against the screen. The steely glint of twilight had begun to show at 04.30 and by now the seas, which *Leviathan* was taking on the nose, were grey-green with dawn.

He glanced at his wristwatch: 05.05 — the R/T was chattering from the wheelhouse. He stared towards the horizon, then heard the distinctive flutter of an approaching helicopter. He heard the 'ting-ting' of the telegraphs, and then the wind's force slowly decreased against the screen.

The chopper was swooping from the lowering cloud. A big machine, its rotor choffing, 'ROYAL NAVY' on its dark-blue fuselage; paint-scarred and salt-caked, it dipped suddenly, then hovered while the pilot judged the relative speed. The roar drowned all else on the bridge and then the machine was bouncing on its floats. Its jets screaming, it debouched its passengers, then lifted into the sky to disappear to the northward. By the time that Jonathan had scrambled down to the upper deck to meet the passengers, the Sea King had vanished.

He would not have recognized David had he not known of his coming. He was already dressed for diving and was carrying his bottles and flippers. Beside him was another diver, smaller but about the same age. Bringing up the rear was the large policeman who must be Assistant Chief Constable Balk; he was prodding Kartar Browne in the back with a pistol.

'David,' Jonathan said, when he had drawn his brother aside, 'I couldn't let you know.'

'Okay, Johnny. Cut the chat. You had a job to do, too...'

His brother hesitated, then followed into the for'ard accommodation superstructure. Jonathan led down the passage, to the lift: 'Fifth deck.' Botsaris was waiting for them on the bridge: the clock showed 05.17.

'We can talk better in my stateroom, gentlemen,' Botsaris said, nodding towards the helmsman and the officer of the watch.

'*Leviathan*'s your ship, isn't she?' Balk asked in the privacy of the cabin. 'Why d'you want to sink her, Mr Browne?'

Browne, in a tweed suit, a silk stock at his neck, stuck his hands into his jacket pockets. He glared at the senior police officer; he refused to speak.

'Come, Browne,' Assistant Chief Constable Balk said brusquely. 'We haven't brought you all this way to play games. As far as I know, we've got one-and-three-quarter hours in which to render this ship safe … *am I right?*' Balk stepped close to the self-assured, suave shipping man.

'You can't make me speak,' Browne snapped. 'I should have my lawyer with me.'

Balk tried to restrain David who had forced himself between the two:

'Browne, you bastard,' David was shouting. 'There's only one person here who can save this ship…' He struck his chest with his fist. 'And that's me. But I can't do so unless you tell me when the Mark II charges are due to explode. *When?* He jabbed the smaller man in the chest. '*When*, you bastard, *when?*'

Kartar Browne spat in David's face.

'Right…,' David was wiping off the saliva on his rubber sleeve. 'Right, Browne.' He turned to Balk. 'I'm not diving, sir, until he calls up his henchman, Carlsen. He must hand over Mrs Grant immediately — or I won't go down.'

'Steady, Mr Krivine.' Balk placed a hand on the diver's shoulder, but David angrily flung it off.

Browne was laughing. 'I wanted this ship to sink, you fools. Can't you understand that?'

'You won't get a penny insurance,' Jonathan said.

'You'll go to jail for most of your life.' Balk had stepped up close to the magnate. 'Two can play funny buggers, Browne. You're coming down to the engine-room with us,' Balk snapped as he grabbed Browne's arm.

Browne's self-confidence seemed to flag: 'Down there?' he queried falteringly, resisting the pressure.

'I'm going to rope you to the circulator inlets. We'll see how you like that,' Balk said.

Browne twisted on his heel: 'You can't do that, Balk...' The colour had drained from his face.

'Yes, I bloody well can. Get going.'

'Get me London 794-9074,' Browne shouted. 'I'll talk to Carlsen.'

'Take it in the radio office,' Botsaris said. They were through to Land's End in seconds. The radio officer handed the phone to Browne. 'Press the handle and speak...'

'Carlsen?' Jonathan was watching his brother who was standing tense and white in the doorway, fiddling with the key strung about his neck. Behind him stood the police diver, Brett.

'... yes, Knud, this is Kartar. Release Mrs Grant immediately.'

Balk was listening in on the spare receiver: 'Tell him to take her to the Swiss Cottage police station,' he whispered. 'I'll be phoning them in half an hour. If she's not there...,' and he jabbed his gun viciously into Browne's ribs so that he cried out with pain.

'No, Knud. There's no alternative — do as I say.' He added, 'My life's at stake too, Knud ... half an hour, so get a move on.'

David snapped from the doorway:

'Thanks, Mr Balk. Stop the ship. Can you give me a lee on the starboard side, please Captain? Mr Brett and I are going down. Can you lower us in the basket to save time?' He turned to the mate who had joined them from the bridge. 'Can you rig bottom lines for us please, as rapidly as possible?'

'Where, Mr Krivine? This is a big ship...'

'First, at station B, abreast tanks Y3 and Y4. You'll see the traces of a white line on her side which we left after cleaning. Then another at D15 and D16, if you can.' He turned to Brett. 'Handle the lamp for me, Jim. I'll see to the monitors.' David spun round suddenly. He grabbed Browne by the neck, shaking him like a terrier with a rat.

'If, by the time we surface, you haven't told 'em what time the Mark IIs are due to go off, I'll wring your bloody neck.' David flung the man down, then slammed the door behind him.

Browne lay in the corner, beneath the main transmitter. His frightened eyes were following the red second-hand on the clock above Sparks' desk: 05.34... Jonathan was watching Kartar Browne's twitching face.

'My God!' Jonathan shouted at Balk. 'Those Mark IIs in the engine-room could go off *before* the Mark Is.' He turned on Browne who was staggering to his feet:

'And my brother's gone down,' he shouted at him. 'When are the Mark IIs due to explode?'

Browne said nothing as he dusted off his suit. Balk had turned to Botsaris: 'You're stopping the ship, Captain?'

'The way is coming off her now.'

'Can someone please take Mr Krivine down to the condenser and circulator inlets?'

'Yes ... certainly.' The master was shaking his head. 'Mr Krivine, perhaps *you* can make Browne talk? Lashing him to the condenser inlet valve might encourage him.'

'There's a rope in the engine-room,' the chief engineer said. 'I'll take you down.'

'I'll stay with the captain,' Balk said. 'We've a decision to make: there's not much time.'

CHAPTER 24

Captain Giorgios Botsaris rubbed his eyes as he watched *Leviathan*'s bow begin to swing to starboard across the grey horizon. It was already 05.37 and the grey dawn was merging with the advancing day. He could not accept that these swift-moving events were taking place on board his magnificent ship. He was irritated by the arrogance of this policeman behind him.

'I'm sorry, Captain,' Balk was saying. 'I think you should leave your ship temporarily.'

Botsaris continued to stare through the curved glass windows of his wheelhouse. 'I do so under protest. You will have to take responsibility if there are any accidents to my crew. Look at the weather, Commandant!'

'Course, sir,' the helmsman reported, '310°. Ship has lost steerage way.'

Leviathan was rolling sedately, beam-on to the seas. Botsaris was watching the crane driver plumbing the basket for the police diver and the manager of Hull Cleaning Services: the gear seemed to be giving them trouble, as they manned the conical rope basket. The mate was on the fo'c'sle-head with the watch-on-deck, trying to slip the bottom lines over the bulb.

'We should not have long in the boats,' Balk was adding. 'The navy'll be here directly.'

'Ever been away in a seaway in a lifeboat, Commander?' Botsaris turned to contemplate the self-assured policeman in front of him.

'It so happens, Captain, I have. I was in the navy off Seoul during the winter of the Korean war.' He added, 'To reassure you, I suggest we call up *Audacity*. She can pass us her ETA for her rendezvous with us.'

It was 05.41 and events were out of Botsaris's control now; let the fellow get on with it. Then *Audacity* came on the air, her captain speaking directly with Balk. The frigate had been forced to reduce speed off Start Point, able to make good only twenty-eight knots in the head sea. At 07.00 she expected to be still seventeen miles from *Leviathan*: over half an hour. No, she had not yet raised *Leviathan* on her radar. A Sea King would be replacing her off Start to help the yacht in difficulties.

'I wondered why the chopper left in such a hurry,' Balk said as he put down the mike. 'Captain, we'll lose nothing by leaving the ship. It's a sensible precaution.'

'You're right, of course, Commandant,' Botsaris admitted wearily. 'The chief engineer will have to shut down his circulators, anyway, for the divers.'

Balk had moved to the HF again. Land's End was coming through on Channel *Zero*.

'Yes, Balk here: Assistant Chief Constable... Swiss Cottage Constabulary? Yes ... yes. Thank the inspector ... *out*.'

Botsaris glanced at the clock: had half an hour passed already? Balk had slipped to the Engine-Room Consol and had picked up the phone; he was watching on the television monitor the two figures moving like marionettes by the port condenser and circulator inlet valve. Botsaris joined him, fascinated by the drama being played out down there. Though pinioned by the-rope, Kartar Browne was shrugging his shoulders. Krivine seemed to be getting nowhere with him — and then the Lloyd's man was jerking round to snatch the phone from its bracket.

'Don't give anything away to Browne,' Balk told him quietly. 'But Swiss Cottage have just been through; they've got Mrs Grant safely in the station.'

The tall, thin man in the engine-room glanced at the TV screen above him. Then he turned and rejoined the figure bound to the massive valve-box on the ship's side. There was more gesticulating, but it was obvious that Browne was still refusing to talk. Botsaris felt better; at last something had gone their way.

The ship's automatic clock bell was striking four bells when the white, overalled figure of the chief engineer pushed through the door at the rear of the bridge.

'Thanks, Chief,' Balk said. 'Browne's not happy, I gather.'

The chief engineer smiled bleakly. 'Not so keen myself,' he said, 'to be within a metre of a time-bomb ticking away beneath me, on the other side of the plating: it doesn't appeal — I'm too old, I guess...'

Botsaris had always got on well with his chief engineer, a dour man, devoted to his Martian engine-room. He wasn't going to like what was coming to him: 'I'm abandoning ship,' the master said. 'No panic — we'll lie off in the boats until the danger's over.'

The chief scratched his crinkly, greying hair. 'You're serious, Captain?'

Botsaris jerked his head towards Balk. 'He insists. He's right; we owe it to the crew.'

'If you say so, Captain.' The chief moved to the Telecommand Consol: 'I never thought I would ever have to scram the reactors for real.' He jabbed at the two red buttons. 'The rods should withdraw,' he said simply. 'Providing they do, whatever happens to the ship, the reactors shouldn't run wild.' He glanced at the TV monitors: 'Now for the boilers.' He touched the two green switches to start the shutting-down programme ... the sprayers ... *and the inlets*...? His finger was poised over the last two pushes, when he glanced at the master: 'D'you think, Captain, there really is a risk of an explosion in the cofferdams?'

'Why?'

'If I shut the hull inlet valves, the tamping effect of the explosion could be worse than if I leave the valves open.'

'Assume the worst,' Balk interrupted. 'If nothing happens, Chief, we'll have lost nothing.'

'I'll leave 'em open then.' He turned to Botsaris: 'Well, Captain, your ship's immobilized.' His eyebrows were raised quizzically.

'Man the port lifeboat, Chief,' Botsaris said. 'I'll take the starboard.' He was moving towards the wings when the mate arrived breathless on the bridge. 'The bottom lines are rigged, sir. The ladders are over the side. Who's going to man the crane for the divers, when we leave the ship?'

The officer of the watch, Paul Usoko, was standing behind them. 'I'll take care of the divers, Captain.'

Botsaris nodded, then walked slowly towards the starboard door. 'Which boat will you take, Commandant?' he asked.

'I'm staying here,' Balk said. 'I'll join you later.'

'Sound the alarm,' the master ordered, glancing at Usoko. '*Abandon ship*...'

CHAPTER 25

'We're on our own now,' Jonathan Krivine yelled above the scream of the turbo-generators, 'and I'm keeping you lashed here until you tell me when the Mark II charges are due to explode.'

'On our own?' Browne asked sarcastically, as his eyes swept towards the TV screen angled on the bulkhead above them.

Krivine ignored him. 'Why do you persist, Browne?' He tapped the inlet casing. 'You can never collect the insurance.'

Browne had opened his mouth, when suddenly the vast room was filled by the blaring of the ship's alarm system: six long blasts, followed by six more, continuously. Browne tried to raise his hands from his bonds to stop his ears.

'*Abandon ship, abandon ship, abandon ship...*'

'That's Paul Usoko,' Jonathan said. 'Bloody good officer...' and he peered at the clock above the watchkeeper's desk: *three minutes past six.*

God, David had guts ... Jonathan did not envy him or the police diver, swimming at this moment under the ship's bottom, searching for the charges ... and then Jonathan realized that the alarm had stopped. Browne was shouting at him and his eyes were wild.

'Will you guarantee me and my wife a free pardon if I tell you?' he asked. 'Come on, Krivine, let me go, for Christ's sake. We haven't much time. It's nearly a quarter past...'

'Okay. Let's have it.'

'Swear to my pardon. Guarantee it...'

'I can't do that.' Jonathan hurried to the phone. 'Mr Balk?'

'Yes?'

'Browne is cracking. He'll talk if you guarantee him a free pardon.'

There was a short pause. 'Tell him to go to hell. I won't be blackmailed. Hold on, Mr Krivine ... the Nigerian officer is waving from the crane ... I think your brother's just surfacing.' The phone went dead.

Jonathan returned to Kartar Browne. The man was broken. His words were barely intelligible. 'Listen, Krivine.' Saliva was drooling from the corners of his mouth; his eyes were wild. Beads of sweat mottled his forehead. 'These Mark IIs here have different settings. Tell your brother not to waste time amidships.' He was pleading, his fingers in spasms as they stretched towards Jonathan. 'Tell him to move aft, here. For God's sake ... *let me go. You can't...*'

But Jonathan had slithered across the plates to the telephone. The clock was showing 06.17.

'Balk? Tell David to move aft — not to waste time amidships. Browne's cracked.'

'I'm on my own here, Krivine. The boats are away. I can't communicate with your brother,' and the policeman's voice faded. Jonathan slammed the instrument back into its rest. He began racing up the ladder. 'I'll be back,' he yelled at Browne over his shoulder. 'I'll tell my brother myself.'

Kartar Browne was yelling frantically behind him: '...bloody fools ... you can't make both batches safe, Krivine. There's no time...' Tears were streaming down his cheeks as he screamed: 'Whoever said that these cofferdam Mark IIs would explode *after* seven o'clock? You bloody, bloody idiots.'

Jonathan had reached the airlock. He must reach the upper deck directly above David, before his brother dipped again. As he pushed open the screen door, his watch was showing twenty-one minutes past six.

As David followed Brett towards the surface he felt once again for the key tied around his neck: he would have forgotten it without the lanyard. By the light of Brett's lamp, they had followed down the bottom line and located the two Mark I devices, Y3 and Y4. He had slipped the key into the keyway and carefully turned the switch to 'off'. An unpleasant moment...

Brett's legs were threshing above him. Then David was also on the surface, pushing off from the red side which was towering over them and slowly rolling in the surging sea. He saw the basket, swinging several metres above their heads, the basket in which Usoko had lowered them so much more quickly than if they had climbed down the pilot ladders which the mate had slung over the side at both stations. If only Brett and he could take time for a breather... He lifted his wrist and his heart stopped a beat: already 06.19.

And then he saw the lifeboat wallowing in the swell, some distance off the ship: orange sides and overloaded, by the look of her ... someone was standing up and pointing in the stern — could have been the Greek captain, Botsaris. Bloody awful time the oarsmen were keeping... Looked like a broken-down windmill, the way they were flailing their oars. The engine probably wouldn't start.

Brett was staring upwards towards the upper deck.

'We won't waste time, Jim,' David gasped through his visor. 'Straight to the midship line.' He rolled over, began kicking steadily towards the stern. It would take a few minutes to reach station D...

As he floated upon his back, he caught sight of someone scrambling along the guard rails. He paused a moment, shoved

197

back his mask. As his eyes focused, he recognized Johnny …
his brother was waving and pointing aft.

'Impatient idiot,' David muttered. 'We're doing the best we
can.' He drove hard with his legs — the rope was almost
within reach now. He waved upwards towards Jonathan,
slipped on his mask, then signalled Brett to precede him down
the bottom line. His watch was reading 06.22 — plenty of air
in hand — but thank God they were not at depth. This was an
impossible race against time — but, what the hell, if he was
blown to bits? 'Great hero attempts to save ship… Lloyd's
medal…'

If he got a move on, and concentrated, he might make the
after two Mark IIs as well, before seven o'clock. Brett's legs
were weaving rhythmically in front of him in the wavering light
… he was following the bottom line when they came upon the
first of the Mark IIs. He shook his head; he would leave these
until after he had set the Mark Is to safe … and then Brett had
found D15. The plastic pod gleamed in the beam of the lamp.
It was still fixed. He twitched up to the pod and slipped the
key into the keyway … *steady*, anti-clockwise … 'off' … and
now on to the next. Ignoring the central Mark II, they traced
D16 and repeated the performance.

Brett held up his thumb and was grinning behind his mask
— a bit of luck to have such a good man as this to help…
David signalled for him to continue across to port until they
found the outboard Mark II. All they could do was to knock
the switches off. If David could manage it, he would try to
break the charges free: they would sink to the bottom.

Brett's lamp was focusing onto the port Mark II: it had not
shifted. Glistening in the beam, it looked particularly sinister
and unpleasant, now that David realized it was full of

explosive. He lifted his hand towards the switch. He felt it give, registered 'off'. Now to wrench it free from the hull.

He paddled with his legs, trying to keep close to the hull. He wrapped the crooks of his arms about the pod. He wrenched, twisted, pulled with all his strength...

He pushed himself clear, took Brett's lamp. He watched as the diver yanked at it ... the water swirled but the charge would not budge. He tapped Brett on the shoulder, passed him the lamp, and signalled for him to return along the bottom-line: the centre Mark II next.

The egg-shaped device loomed from out of the dark. David switched it to 'off', then they wasted several minutes trying to shift it, but it would not budge. They hurried to the starboard Mark II, switched it to 'off'. The hands of David's watch glowed at *twenty minutes to seven*.

He pointed upwards and began threshing his way to the surface.

CHAPTER 26

When Jonathan finally returned at 06.26 to the engine-room, after his abortive attempt to contact David, he found Kartar Browne almost insane: saliva was frothing at the corners of his mouth and his eyes bulged.

'You're not going to let me drown? You can't … you … I'll tell you and then…' Jonathan had never before seen a completely broken man: Browne's hands were beating feebly upon the casing. 'Stop — listen, Krivine. Listen to me — I'll tell…' His eyes rolled. 'Here — *here*,' he screamed. 'These Mark IIs will explode a quarter of an hour *before* the others. *Before*, do you hear? These, and the Mark IIs amidships, are time fused; but they contain a secondary action, in case the time mechanism fails. They can also be triggered by shockwaves, like oyster mines. Can't you understand, Krivine? If these fail *here*,' and he beat the casing again, 'they'll be exploded by the shock from the midship charges, whether from the Mark Is or IIs.'

Jonathan drew in his breath: 'You thought of everything.'

A glint of cunning showed in Browne's eyes. 'Ah, Krivine,' he was wiping the saliva with the back of his hand, 'but the Mark IIs at D section are time-set to explode fifteen minutes *after* seven o'clock, in case the shock mechanism fails.' He began laughing hysterically, as he writhed in his bonds.

'Let me go — please, Krivine, oh, please, Mr Krivine, can't…'

But Jonathan had been watching the time: it was already 06.35. He might just catch David as he surfaced from his dive amidships. So long as he did not proceed immediately aft underwater — Jonathan rushed up the ladder, leaving the screaming maniac behind him. Browne was not fooling: the after Mark II charges in the cofferdams would be exploding at 06.45 — fifteen minutes *before* the earliest estimated time. He must, at all costs, prevent Dave from diving again; he could not possibly set the after charges safe before 07.00.

He felt the wind in his face as he raced, slithering and stumbling along the upper deck. The Nigerian officer was running towards him from the crane. He saw the pilot's ladder, twenty yards away. He reached it, then swung himself over the rail. The sea was swilling against her red sides, as she rolled majestically in the swell; away to starboard a lifeboat was lying off — and he began scrambling down the wooden slats of the ladder, down towards the sea eighty feet below. Balk must have seen him from the bridge, must have guessed. Then Jonathan heard a man shouting below him from the sea... David was calling up to him.

'Dave — Dave — *Stay where you are!* He held on by one hand, and looked down over his shoulder. David was wallowing on his back in the swell; the police diver was breaking surface alongside him.

'*David — Stop! Stay where you are...*'

His brother's legs kicked and then one hand lifted to grab the ladder. Seconds later, Jonathan had reached him: 'David, what's the time?'

Twisting his wrist, his brother snapped: '06.39 — about twenty minutes to go. We can manage it, if you don't bloody well interfere,' and he began to push off from the ship's side. Jonathan grabbed him by an air bottle.

'The Mark IIs in the cofferdams are set to go off a quarter of an hour earlier ... *at 06.45, David.*'

'...four and a half minutes?'

'Yes.'

'*Bloody hell!*'

'And David…'

'Yeah…?' His face was drained of colour behind his mask.

'Sally's safe.'

David glared; his mouth twitched. 'Thanks.' He yelled to the police diver: 'Swim to the lifeboat, Jim.' He tapped him on the shoulder and pointed to starboard. 'The lifeboat. *Get moving, boy…*' He turned towards his brother.

'What about Browne?' he shouted. 'Can't let the bugger drown like a rat…' He was hauling himself from the water and wrenching off his flippers which splashed into the sea. Jonathan heard David panting beneath him, as they hauled themselves hand over hand up the ladder. Usoko was waiting for them at the gunwale; Jonathan grabbed his walkie-talkie: 'Balk,' he gasped into the mike. 'Mr Balk. We're going down for Browne. For God's sake, get over the side yourself. The ship's going up at 06.45…'

Jonathan waited several precious seconds, but there was no reply. David and he began racing aft, towards the after island. They were reaching the screen door, when the deck shivered suddenly beneath their feet. Jonathan slithered to a halt. David crashed into him and they both fell as an explosion shattered the world about them. They were hurled against the screen, the breath knocked from their lungs. Then the terrifying silence which followed was punctuated by a succession of rumblings and detonations from below. In seconds, the after part had begun to go down by the stern and was listing to starboard. As they crawled to the doorway, there was a blinding flash before Jonathan's eyes, his surroundings began gyrating about him and he knew no more.

CHAPTER 27

His rubber suit saved him; he was shocked but never lost consciousness. He shook his head, heard the scream of machinery running wild somewhere below. Then the safety-valves lifted, the roar from the vents deafening him as the plumes of condensing super-heated steam drifted away on the wind. As he clambered to his feet, he saw his brother sprawled against the coaming of the starboard winch.

He rolled the unconscious body on to its back. Jonathan's eyes were closed; his face was grey and blood oozed from a gash across his forehead and the bridge of his nose. This was no time for first-aid: the ship was down by the stern already and listing to starboard. Lifejackets… Propping Jonathan against the winch, David hauled himself along the handrail to the screen door.

Inside the after superstructure, the only light was filtering through a half-opened door at the end of the passage. He slithered in his bare feet down the passageway, flinging open the office door; no sign of a lifejacket.

The first touch of panic twitched at him: he felt trapped in here. Then he saw the red arrow pointing for'ard: MUSTER STATION. Balancing against the list, he was reaching a cross-passage when he spotted someone on the central staircase. The man was bent double, heaving and jerking at something he was trying to haul up the steps.

'*Balk!*' David slithered to a halt on the open landing where a stock of orange lifejackets bulged from their overhead stowage.

'Give us a hand.' Balk was shifting his grip beneath the shoulders of a slumped body. 'Only the starboard charge went off,' Balk gasped. 'I was shielded by a fan casing, but Browne caught the full blast. Water's flooding in like a deluge: up to the plates when I got out.'

Kartar Browne looked dead, his face pallid with the touch of death. David hauled out five jackets, giving two to Balk who slipped one on himself. He began sliding one over Browne's head, as David pushed open the screen door. Jonathan was staggering towards them. David steadied him, slipping an arm beneath his armpits.

'Follow me to the ladder,' he bawled at Balk, above the roar of the escaping steam. 'Too dicey to jump from here.'

He reached the open deck when he realized that Jonathan was trying to make himself heard: 'I'm all right now, Dave. I can manage.'

David raced back to help Balk. Browne's body was sliding more easily along the greasy deck. 'Take the legs,' Balk barked. 'We'll have to rope him down the ladder. I'm not certain he's dead.'

'It's just coming up to seven o'clock,' David yelled. 'We can sling him over. If there's any life in him, he'll stand a chance.'

At the ladder, David took charge: 'The Mark Is are going up underneath us any minute.'

David crouched over the body, firmly secured the tapes of Browne's lifejacket. He took the feet, Balk the torso.

'*One*,' said David. '*Two…*'

'*Three…*,' yelled Balk.

They heaved together. Browne's body sailed over the side and vanished. They rushed for the ladder and began scrambling down the side.

'There they are, sir…'

Paul Usoko was standing alongside Captain Botsaris in the sternsheets of the starboard lifeboat. After the explosion the Nigerian had taken to the sea; though without a lifejacket he had followed the police diver Brett, who, hearing Usoko's shouts, had waited for him.

'*There*, Captain — by the island — making for the ladder…'

The orange-coloured, glass-fibre lifeboat was wallowing in the sea, lying off, a cable clear. No one spoke, each man mesmerized by the pygmies still moving along *Leviathan*'s upper deck.

One figure (to Usoko, it resembled Jonathan Krivine) had already reached the pilot's ladder. The other two (from their size, unmistakably David Krivine and the big policeman) were humping a sagging body along the upper deck.

Captain Botsaris checked the time. 'Three minutes…' he was muttering to himself.

'They're directly above D section,' Usoko said.

They watched the body being hove over the side. They saw it splash as it hit the water. Botsaris was crossing himself: 'It's Kartar Browne,' he said softly.

He threw the gear-lever to 'ahead', knocked up the revs to 'full'. 'Stand by to pick 'em up,' he commanded. 'Paul, keep an eye on the body, while I handle the boat.' He slogged the lifeboat in at full speed, swooping in beneath the ladder. The three men jumped, one after the other. They did not wet their feet.

'Bowman — bear off…'

Botsaris slammed over the tiller; the lifeboat surged ahead, swung off to starboard. He kicked up the throttle.

'Lie down in the boat,' he called. 'Those who can.' He turned his back resolutely upon his ship. He kept the lifeboat at full throttle, opening the distance with every second that passed. Half-a-mile distant, they fitfully caught sight of the other lifeboat, bobbing in the swell.

David struggled to his feet in the cramped space, splayed his legs. He peered at his watch: 07.15 precisely. Like the others, he was holding his breath and watching; staring in silence at the stricken ship.

Leviathan had settled by the stern, her poop awash, the seas breaking white against the after island. She had listed to starboard and David could recognize the blue interior of the stern swimming pool. Steam was no longer blasting from her safety valves, but the seas around her transom were boiling and leaping in confusion.

Her enormous length emphasized the angle she had taken on: fifteen degrees bow-up. Her bulb could now be forty feet above the surface of the sea.

'If the engine-room bulkhead holds,' Botsaris was saying, 'she might keep afloat.'

'If she doesn't slide stern first,' David said. 'The engine-room is a gigantic compartment to be flooded.'

'She's plenty of buoyancy for'ard and...' But David never caught the remainder of Botsaris's sentence.

At the point where her bottom emerged from the sea the water suddenly heaved, began to froth. At the same instant, a succession of explosions, almost instantaneous, hammered against the bottom of the lifeboat.

'My God...' Botsaris whispered.

A V-shaped rent was opening slowly in *Leviathan*'s side. Beginning on the upper deck abaft the crane it gradually opened until David could see the sky through the far side of the ship. As it widened, the tortured noises of buckling, twisting metal reached the occupants of the lifeboat.

'She's splitting down the middle,' Balk was saying softly. 'That colossal weight right forward and the engine-room full of water.'

David remembered the wartime cruiser, the museum ship in the Thames — *Belfast* wasn't she? She had sat on a mine in the Forth and had broken her back in the same way — weakness in a new design, he'd been told. Balk was right; he usually was.

Tears were streaming down Botsaris's cheeks. He stood in the sternsheets, hands by his side, mesmerized... The fearful cacophony of rending steel continued until the for'ard half of the ship splashed back into the boiling cauldron of the ocean. She rocked there for a few moments, then slowly settled, bow-down, the mangled section poking just above the sea.

Usoko was pointing to the northward. Above the horizon, David saw the white pedestal mast of a warship. She was steaming fast and growing larger at every second. The spray was flying high, sweeping over her, casting a veil over her bridge.

EPILOGUE

Audacity's captain was peering through his binoculars at the stricken hulk: 'I've never seen a ship go to the bottom,' the young commander murmured. 'My father was in the Battle of the Atlantic. He told me there was no more terrible sight.'

David Krivine was standing by his side. 'My old man said the same thing,' he added quietly. 'Nothing worse.' With blankets thrown about them, he, Jonathan and *Leviathan*'s surviving officers were huddled in *Audacity*'s port wings: for over half an hour they had been watching the fore-part of the great ship wallowing beam-on to the seas. Ocean tugs were racing to her position, but she was much lower in the water now: she was listing to starboard and the jagged, macerated after-section was open to the battering from the Atlantic rollers breaking over her. David needed a few moments respite: he quietly withdrew from the silent watchers and moved across to *Audacity*'s starboard side.

He could see his father so vividly, could remember so clearly that evening by his study fireside: the crackling logs, the reflections of the flames flickering on the ceiling. 'There's something terrible in the way a ship dies,' his father had said. 'She takes a bit of you with her on her final plunge: something fundamental about it — gets at the root of your guts.' This was the evening when Dad had yarned about *his* war, the only occasion he had spoken without reserve of his nightmare... David and Jonathan had come home on leave together as young sub-lieutenants, the last time they had all three been together. David could hear now his father's restrained, matter-of-fact voice...

Jocelyn Krivine had been twenty-one, a lieutenant RNVR, in one of the two 'Counties' which had been caught by the Japanese battlefleet that had swept into the Indian Ocean after the fall of Singapore. Overwhelmed by over fifty carrier aircraft, *Cornwall* and her consort, *Dorsetshire*, had sunk within a few minutes of each other, 424 lives being lost. *Cornwall*'s ship's company was abandoning ship, her men scrambling over her side as she sank. Lieutenant Jocelyn Krivine, one of the last to leave, was picking his way through the twisted metal, when he heard an agonized cry from beneath a heap of tangled steel. Jocelyn was horrified to see a sailor, half his side blown away.

'Shoot me, sir, for God's sake...'

Lieutenant Krivine pulled the revolver from his holster webbing. Pressing the barrel to the side of the man's head, he pulled the trigger. Then he walked over the side and into the sea. He was in the water for twenty-four hours, before he was picked up by the light cruiser, *Enterprise*. His flesh, saturated by the warm water, fell off his body in lumps.

'I'll never forget the gratitude in the man's eyes,' his father had murmured by the fireside. 'But I've been haunted by my action ever since...' He had drawn the evening to a close with the remark: 'There's no more terrible sight than a sinking ship.'

David Krivine shook his head, dragged himself back to the present. *And Sally?* During this last hectic hour he had put her out of his mind — how had she fared, how would he find her? Would the police take her back to Trefusis? All that mattered was that she was safe, thank God. They would eventually pick up Carlsen... Reluctantly David rejoined the others who had moved to the deck abaft *Audacity*'s bridge.

'She's settling fast,' Jonathan said.

The mangled cross-section of *Leviathan*'s hulk was subsiding beneath the surface, the seas surging through the tangled, twisted steel. *Audacity* was lying off at half a mile, but even at this distance, David could hear the rumble of underwater explosions as the tanker's bulkheads collapsed. For another twenty minutes the process continued: whorls of escaping air boiled to the surface, spurting high, then drifting to leeward in curtains of cascading spray.

Slowly she was taking on a steeper bow-up angle, until she was hanging almost vertically, two thirds of her fore-section now beneath the waves. Her Wellsian bridge structure, so impressive when she had floated to her marks, was now canted vertically, her scimitar mast parallel with the horizon. Her Panamanian flag, fouled around the halyards, hung limply, fluttering no more. Then, with a final rush, she began to go…

The gigantic prow, its bulb thrusting into the sky, hung for an interminable moment, glistening above the red hull. Suddenly the foremast thrashed into the sea, disappeared, water spurting upwards through the bridge doors and ports, in jets of flying spume…

Convulsed in her last throes, the ocean heaved, seemed to part to receive its sacrifice: the bridge vanished beneath the boiling surface; the starboard anchor cable dangled like a watch chain from its navel pipe and huge windlass; then her stem was smothered in a mist of spume, until only the glistening neb of the bulb remained…

She was gone. The horizon stretched unbroken, save for the hump of threshing water where the air gobs broke the surface in monstrous, frothing blisters.

They stood in shocked silence abaft *Audacity*'s bridge, until long after she had vanished. An oil drum and a few baulks of timber bobbing in the curling seas were the only traces left of the largest ship in the world. Above *Leviathan*'s grave, a motley of gulls and Molly birds wheeled and screeched in excited anticipation.

David broke the silence: 'Well, Johnny,' he said. 'It's back to your Lloyd's box now: you'll have a thing or two to tell 'em.'

The Surveyor's Supplementary Report Submitted to Underwriters
The frigate, *Audacity*, arrived on the scene of the disaster twelve minutes after NSS *Leviathan* split into two. After picking up the survivors of the port lifeboat, *Audacity* was crossing astern of the remaining half-section of *Leviathan*, when she nearly ran down a survivor floating with his back to the seas, his head held upright by his orange lifejacket. The man was barely conscious but he recovered sufficiently to be transferred to hospital when the frigate returned to Plymouth. The survivor was identified as Mr Kartar Browne.

Audacity then went alongside *Leviathan*'s starboard lifeboat. Amongst the survivors were the master of the ship, Captain Giorgios Botsaris; his third officer, Mr Paul Usoko; the assistant chief constable, Commander Charles Balk; the managing director of Hull Cleaning Services, Mr David Krivine; a police diver, Mr James Brett; and a Lloyd's special surveyor, Mr Jonathan Krivine. After medical examination in the Royal Naval Hospital, Plymouth, all members of the crew were discharged; no nuclear contamination is suspected.

Audacity lay off the remaining section of *Leviathan* until it sank at 11.28 in position 253° — Ushant Lt — seventy-nine miles, in ninety-five fathoms. The ship, by good fortune, was outward bound to the Persian Gulf and was in ballast. Oil pollution will not be serious but it is feared that her tank bulkheads may have collapsed.

At the time of writing this report (17 August) it is not known whether Planeka Shipping International Ltd, will press its insurance claim, but a formidable legal confrontation is impending. Those involved are The Crown, Lloyd's Corporation, Mr Kartar Browne, and Planeka Shipping International Ltd. It is understood that Mr Browne is being charged for attempted fraud; and, with his operations manager, Mr Knud Carlsen, for the murder of Mr Alfred Kelway, an employee of Hull Cleaning Services Ltd. Mr Browne, in refuting the accusations, is counter-charging the police, and Mr Jonathan Krivine, for attempted murder. While these lawsuits await judgment (a process which may drag on for years) the radioactive pollution from *Leviathan*'s four nuclear-reactors continues.

Though the sunken ship lies nearer to France, the south coast of England may be worse affected by the main flood stream and the weather carrying the pollution further up-Channel. Because this menace affects both nations, rapid decisions are inevitably difficult to achieve. While the politicians of both countries mouth their platitudes, *Leviathan*'s reactors continue to simmer on the seabed, because her reactors failed to 'scram'. Why there was a malfunction will remain a mystery until her machinery can be inspected. It will be a courageous diver or submersible crew who will risk their lives in approaching this radioactive machinery.

Unless a massive (and successful) Anglo-French salvage operation is rapidly mounted, the nuclear pollution will continue to infect the south-western approaches to the Channel for a long time to come. The effects on the British and French fishing and shell-fishing industries, already decimated by oil-pollution and by the lack of conservancy control, may be calamitous. It is not known what the resulting damage will be to our lobster, mussel, prawn and shrimp trade.

Is it possible that the Channel may become a dead sea? The question is formulated before the nightmare becomes reality.

The opponents of the ULCC building programmes are confronted by the following arguments:

(a) That two ULCCs are the equivalent of four VLCCs of 250,000 tons; or eleven tankers of 100,000 tons; or seventy tankers of 16,000 tons. Numerically, therefore, the collision risk is proportionally reduced if ULCCs replace smaller tankers. Similarly, costs are relatively lower.

(b) These gigantic ships are as near safe as man can make them; because of their technical excellence, both in machinery, in navigational and communication equipment, they should never break down or become involved in a collision situation.

The protagonists for a limitation in tanker size point out that, while ships ply the oceans with man in command, there will always be accidents; that the larger the ship, the greater the potential catastrophe.

It is criminal, the protagonists aver, to jeopardize our environment merely because economics demand big ships. Can the case really be defended, they ask, for monster ships to be built? Can humanity accept the risk of half a million tons of crude oil floating in an eighteen-knot motorized barge upon the surface of the sea?

Should the size of tankers (or ships with lethal capability) be limited by international law? Should their size be controlled, relative to their damage potential? Should a traditionally propelled ship be permitted to be larger than her nuclear-powered sister?

'There must come a limit,' they said. 'One million tons.' The *Leviathan* tragedy will perhaps make owners and their experts pause before launching even larger ships.

For how long will those pulsing reactors, their radioactivity borne upon the surge of the flood stream, continue to pollute our seas? For how many years will this nuclear poison continue, destroying and deforming the miraculous biological balance of the marine life around our sceptred isle? Man's progress must be weighed against the cost.

JONATHAN KRIVINE
Lethbridge and Seymour Underwriters

A NOTE TO THE READER

Dear Reader,

If you have enjoyed the novel enough to leave a review on **Amazon** and **Goodreads**, then we would be truly grateful.

Sapere Books is an exciting new publisher of brilliant fiction and popular history.

To find out more about our latest releases and our monthly bargain books visit our website:
saperebooks.com

Printed in Great Britain
by Amazon